Cara's Tale of Wolves and Freedom
  Copyright 2007 by Kay Hazel
ISBN # 978-0-6151-7839-4
  First Edition
Copyright 2007 Chelsea Pubs Publishing Company

~For the few out there who understand what it means when I say, "Resist domestication". I love you all, always believe in yourself. Also to my mother, my grandmother, and Kuhappi. All of you inspired me greatly and I am forever in thanks. ~

CARA'S TALE OF

WOLVES   AND

FREEDOM

Introduction
~~~~~~~~~~~~~~~~~~~~~~~~~

When a child is born, an entire world is opened up to
them. Some little bodies are not yet ready, others have been

waiting for so long great things are bound to happen, and happen fast. Growing up in repression and longing, she always wished to be somewhere else...

When destiny and fate often have their way and, being normal no longer remains an option. This is the background to an amazing tale. This is just the introduction. This is the beginning of Cara Sedalia's story.

The Beginning

Prologue

Memory started at a tender age for Cara. She remembered her childhood only as one remembers an exhausting dream. Detailed images, only the most climactic events, and no real details of how or why the dream occurred. The dream was the most accurate description of how she had grown up. Looking back, her past had always been one that never quite matched up to who she had grown to be. That was at least what she thought. A lot had happened. It seemed to have no reason. Little did she know it was those same seemingly meaningless events that had equipped her with skills and knowledge to prevail in the world that lay ahead.

Cara grew up as an only child, a socially inept one at that. Her days were spent at school or in a church with her family. They did not live together but were sprawled out across some valley town paved in cement. Enriching, stimulating. Not.

In school, she never really played with the other children. Not because she was slow or retarded, nor was she at the other end of that scale. Little Miss Sedalia was never the "gifted" child who was too smart to play with dolls and jacks and in return, got special access to books and activities that her own young mind craved for. Those kinds of kids made her young body hot with frustrations and annoyance, simply with their presence. They had no imaginations and could never play alone. She on the other hand, was her own best friend. No, she just never fit in it seemed, especially not at home.

Strike one, the big-eyed little girl had no real interest in learning the bible stories her parents tried to bring her up on. They were the same stories their parents grew up on, and the generations before them. It wasn't that they were written poorly, even if they had been originally, by this time they'd been re-told and re-published so many times that they had been made to sound good. Surly and obviously they did to most, over half the nation at the minimum. But to her, they just weren't that creative. Well that is except for the one about the lion's den, or the one about the ark and all the creatures, wild and untamed. She liked hearing about the animals, but that was about it.

Strike two; her shyness and resistance when it came to making friends and "playing nice". That was when her parents used children's friendship to one up the prosperous neighbor or accountant next door. She always failed to be proper and when tax day came, it would hit harder than the year before.

The Sedalia family couldn't have pets. It was always too much money or too much hassle, the parental explanation varied by the day. Though never once did it matter, excuses mean nothing to a child. Instead Cara got the famous,

"Why don't you just play with the puppy next door?"

Going next door just wasn't the same as having a friend of her own to share her life with. All she wanted was someone to guide, to talk to and, to call her own. After years of begging, and her consistent refusal to go next door, Cara finally stopped asking. Ever after she kept her words numbered and her laughter hushed. That must have been strike three.

So no sleep-over, no youth group, no soccer pals, and certainly no Saturday nights at the mall. Yet she felt this as no loss. Her friends were always around to be her company. How? Through the wind, creeks, fields and trees, Cara held her conversations. She spoke with them all; rabbits, voles, songbirds, hawks, owls and even the foxes. In the suburbs, there wasn't much wildlife to be had, though what there was owned her spirit. She spent the majority of her time with them, night and day.

Dad took Cara up to the mountains about twice a year. He had little knowledge of the land but kicked himself out of the house whenever his wife's silverware parties came up. Somehow he'd gather some "hiking buddies" from the office. Together they'd scale a mountain and camp out. In the morning the group would go to brunch at the local mountain town and then drive the speed limit home. All members from breakfast were, of course, in their respective minivans and SUVs.

When Cara was out in the Rocky Mountains, she was in sheer bliss. She always walked half a mile ahead of the bunch where she was able to take in everything without distraction. The captivating views, the lush smells and the soothing sounds. She'd climb trees and swim in lakes while the men and boys read their maps and took a breather. Sometimes they would stop just to mingle. Those times were what seemed to keep her going through life, that momentary freedom and peace.

Each time they'd return home, she'd resume her days of listening to soundscape CDs, lighting pine and forest-scented candles, drawing detailed landscapes and animal portraits, and reading multiple volumes of books on the outdoors, plants, nature, animals, mountain men and survival. Everything of the sort filled her bookshelf for years. The sort she was never taught, and the sort from which her civilized and cultured parents disassociated themselves. Suppose that was strike four.

****

Age fourteen, winter snow had graced the scenery for this particular snow-shoeing trip with the "hiking buddies". They were up a winding trail in northern Colorado. Things had been rough at home the past couple of weeks for Cara. Though her parents had been divorced for a decade, things had started getting worse. Each parent was set to remarry in a year and the fiancées were getting real put out with their future stepchild. It was obvious. So Cara went from one house to another, overhearing each parent's plea with the other for one more weekend without her. They'd say,

"Well it's still your turn. Please? Listen, I'll even take you out to lunch at the end of the week if you keep her."

Ouch.

On top of that, "little miss Sedalia" had finally been kicked out of school for fighting and disrespectful conduct towards her teachers.

Snide remarks and questionings of faith were added into that final parent/ teacher conference. The black sheep, mammas little anti-Christ, the names never ended. Although in front of Daddy's business buddies, Cara was free of the verbal torture. In fact, no one else seemed to care whether or not she followed their faith. Everyone in the community simply presumed her a delinquent and treated her accordingly.

Dad would skirt the subjects of her school and religion to avoid crumbling the Sedalia family's reputation. However, her father reminded her hourly how "god damn lucky" she was to be on this trip. That and how she was on "thin ice". Surely no pun was intended there. Regardless, she kept her curvy mouth shut.

Instead of taking up the front on this winter trip, Cara trailed behind. Way behind. Halfway up a hill her father waited for her, while the others rested at the top. When Cara caught up to this emotionally vacant man, her father, he spoke to her in a voice she'd never heard from him use before. He said very quickly and quietly,

"If you DO NOT keep up with us, I WILL leave you behind. I swear Cara Sedalia, at this moment, leaving you behind would be no sweat off my back."

Though he spoke in a whisper, Cara never heard words so loud that they echoed in her rib cage. Each syllable was articulated and annunciated so that she got the full impact of his message. She stood there too stunned to cry. Her father turned his back on her and began shoeing up hill. Fast. Cara stared up to the sky; it was white with layers of winter snow clouds, the kind that make it impossible to tell the time of day. A liquid fire tear burned down the side of her porcelain cheek. Cara shifted her stare now to the top of the hill. Everyone was gone. It was silent. A light snow began to sift from the sky.

So this was it, she thought. Unsurprisingly enough, she wasn't sad, it almost felt like a relief to her. Instead of following the trail up hill, Cara looked to the left, where open hills outlined the waves in the sea of white. To the right, a dense evergreen forest where only a few branches stuck out of the snow blanket. Looking up, as if for guidance, she let out her best wolf -like howl, then headed towards her new home, the forest.

Cara walked for hours and tried to get lost in the woods. The worst thing that could happen now would be her father finding her. He had never beaten her and if he found her, he surely wouldn't hit her, right? At this point she wasn't too sure. The fear of his rage left Cara frozen colder than the weather surrounding her. It made her shiver.

The trunks of the trees spun around her. She no longer knew where she was. She'd only been in these woods once before, a year ago. It all seemed like a brand new world now, a blank white canvas. Above, the sky began to grow a few shades darker. When darkness fell on winter nights such as this, it didn't make much of a difference. The sky seemed to glow warmly, like a 45 watt soft white light bulb. That was good for now; she didn't have the slightest inclination to stop and was too caught up in thought and emotion to feel her own hunger, cold, and exhaustion. All around, the powder snow was beginning to build up. An emerging owl enforced that the evening was finally in effect. Two hours had elapsed from Cara's meeting with her father.

After all her walking, finally there was a break in the firs. Up ahead rose a hill tall enough to be a mountain to a southern man. Realizing she'd have no cover, Cara hustled up the hill, slipping on the loose flour that covered the slope. Legs tingling from the excursion, Cara found herself atop the hill looking out at acres of forest. She hoped no one had spotted her. She wondered where those open hills and the trail had gone. No importance. It was quiet, not a sound but the snow hitting the ground.

She was proud of herself. She had zig zagged her trail and made it through a rough, dense patch of forest. Cara knew they couldn't find her, especially with the snow falling this fast. Even a hound would have a tricky time tracking her. She stretched out on a protruding snow capped boulder, letting the snow melt and roll off her ski coat. Closing her eyes, she re-visited the last scene with her father. After replaying her father's words for a few moments, she threw in flashbacks of her childhood for added affect.

First, she drew up the everlasting pain of her parent's divorce. All her life, Cara was haunted by the feeling that none of it would have happened if it were not for her existence. It was possible her parents could have even been happy together, out in the woods and living their lives. Instead they had her.

Of course there was also the rejection from kids at school, from first grade to her last day in class. More so, her years were filled with times of being told to calm down or else she would break something inside the over decorated house in which her father lived. She hated all the witty small talk avoiding what really mattered, and the stupid movies that filled the hours of dinner, just so no one had to talk. The arguments about nothing, the awful stepparent that up-staged her life and stole the small portion of love Cara felt she deserved. All the eye rolls at the zoos, the fights with teachers at school, the stress, the lies, the loneliness, and the way she managed to be an outcast at every occasion. No one ever shared her passions. No one cared. Well this was it. It was all over.

How anti-climactic. There was no big struggle for this moment to arrive. No blow-out fight, no violence, just a few words had pushed her over the edge. This was nothing like she imagined it to be, but here she was, simply walking away from the pain, she had had enough.

Feeling liquid fire inside her, Cara gave up and released all the anger that simmered inside of her. It evaporated through her pores in the crisp night air. Was this death? She felt empty, with no anger and no passion. It was as if she watched her body go limp beneath her. She seemed to be hovering above her own motionless shell of a body. Suddenly she saw her hand twitch, and her soul was slurped back into its flesh and bones.

She was back. Unsure of reality, Cara bit her thumb hard, and felt her teeth puncture her finger. Releasing, she swallowed her blood and looked to the sky, pain tears filling her eyes. Something moved beneath the boulder she lay upon. She watched, and nothing stirred further.

Clouds were clearing from the sky, as the image of a roaring white tiger filled the sky. She blinked to smear the tears from her eyes. She had to be seeing things. A roar that boomed like thunder rolled across the low-hanging clouds. The image was moving towards her, it was getting bigger. Black out.

One
~~~~~~~~~~~~~~~~~~~~~~~~~~~~~

When Cara woke up she was walking into a dark cave. Her senses returned to her stronger than before. She walked in a body she knew was not her own. Inside the cave, Cara's pupils widened, and she could see again. The white tiger from the sky appeared, sitting at attention in the back of the cave. He spoke not a word, yet Cara seemed to understand what was now at hand. The world was not as it once was.

Blazing visions began immersing themselves inside Cara's memory box. The tiger was casting a slide show of images through her mind to catch her up on the years that had gone by. Watching years of history compressed into flashes and subliminal messages made her nauseous. She wanted to vomit, but couldn't find the focus to even twitch. How had all this happened? So much time had passed. Where had she been? She must have been suspended in time. Her very existence had been paused. The Tiger told her it was for a divine purpose. After pausing to let her vomit, the tiger kept on with the images. The most crucial was yet to come.

Concrete deserts. Fields filled with man-made war along side massive oceans swirling in oil, and rainforests that had been raped and left to die, leaving the stench of death and rotting of bodies in the intense tropical sun. Dead toucan, parrots and birds of every color spotted the terrain like flowers across a meadow. Monkeys, lemurs, bats and insects scattered the empty rolling grounds.

The vast Middle East had become no more than an empty oil mine. Valleys were stripped of their trees and rivers, leaving nothing. No life, not even the lush meadows that once cradled the very beginning of human society. Harsh winds now shaved the hillsides, with no obstacles to dampen their wrath.

Extreme atmospheric changes had occurred without wild forests to release enough oxygen. Carbon monoxide levels were exceptionally high, and breath had been sucked from the planet. Thus, animals existence was not easily supported. Acres of tree stumps and sawdust littered the earth where glorious forests once grew. The few birds that were left, flew around confused and lost. Cara sobbed uncontrollably.

After taking what was desired for trade in man's world, this "virus" would move on. Leaving spots on the earth like dying rashes on a mother's body. As her blood had run dry, the wounds that were left had become unable to heal. Nature was loosing.

Humans reigned as feared, over-populated, sterilized monsters. Creating a race so clean, so bacteria-free, had resulted in a deadly virus that ate away the life of the other living things. This virus was spreading rapidly. The humans that were shown to Cara, were nothing more than drones, unaware to their lethal life stlye as they made their way through their meaningless lives. Cara hoped it was over, yet there was still more.

Like many places in Cara's once native nation, large cities worldwide thrived under a dome of plastic protection from the elements. Beneath the surface were wells of water, and a sewer system that damned up the water from the once connecting oceans and rivers. This left strips of barren land with no resources, and no bio diversity to recreate the balance.

Such places were defined by a never ending skyline of tall buildings, smoke stacks, and acres of churches, malls and various processing plants. America was the leading example for such places, once the largest single emitter of carbon dioxide from the burning of fossil fuels, water pollution from runoff of pesticides and fertilizers, and the human virus thrived with the glory of mass production.

Through all this, there were indeed still a handful of niches and areas where nature had yet prevailed. No more than a few hundred miles at a time, the balance of life managed to defend itself by keeping climates and terrain unbearable for the common human while allowing certain flora and fauna access to evolve and thrive. Places like this smelled sweet, instead of the stench of human sweat and urine.

There will always be light in the midst of darkness, hope lingering in times of unrest. Hidden, there are healers among the killers. Groups of people, foundations, came together in attempt to fight the virus. Most were passive in there defense. However a growing number of outraged men and women grew aggressive, and took matters into their own hands. War had come and gone to the mighty people who enforced their laws of earth and sky. Buckets of blood had been lost. Worst of all, alone in cement jails, men and women had died. Their souls crushed. All this and more served as wicked punishment for upholding their beliefs. Without earth, man could not live, and now without man to protect earth...the results had proven themselves.

Hope was growing for the rebalance of the planet. The men and women who died in the worldwide wars triggered a new nation to form. N.O.T.R. (Nation of the Raven) allowed Canada, Alaska, Greenland, and Iceland to detach completely from the rest of society's modern world and bond politically as one. Surviving members of Native American tribes joined to fulfill life as it once was, and as they believed it should still be. All tribes, immigrants and even locals formed together to create a band of people whose only laws were to them, the ultimate truth of life. Though bands of peoples gathered under different names, all were members of the great Raven Clan.

~ Man is the caretaker of his land. In return the land will take care of mankind.
~ Man is an animal, may he never forget it.
~At the core of the Earth lies one massive brain, giving every form of life purpose, for its existence. One should never question this.
~Existence is free of monopoly charges. Man does not pay another from his own wealth to exist.
~ No national military is supported. Voluntary freedom fighters are restricted to territorial defense only.

Like uncharted waters, this nation was dangerous and unknown to most. N.O.T.R. was self sufficient, using technology to the benefit of the people's planet, rather than a lifestyle luxury. This increased the mystery that shrouded the arctic shores of the unknown nation. What was even more unknown to modern man was the remarkable comeback that the earths, and these people, were making.

Throughout the many different regions of N.O.T.R. wolves sang, birds soared the clear skies, and mountains stood tall, glowing with life. In the oceans, whales played and waves roared upon the shore. Things were different here, the clans worked diligently to solve the serious problems that now threatened all life. Sparing no time, the people attempted creating solutions. No wars, no fees, just a large like-minded nation that, in the end, tallied up with 11,359,857 kilometers of land area.

With an additional 1,940,770 kilometers in protected national waters, a major project was in motion. Advanced filters the size of ships harmlessly floated across the oceans of N.O.T.R. Acting like giant sponges; they absorbed foreign dumped oil and toxins from the ocean and skies. When fully absorbed the oil could then be brought to shore and removed with vacuums, cured and enhanced with local abundant methods, allowing further use. The toxins were disposed of properly. These surfing sponges were just a piece of the ultimate recycling movement that was underway.

The Raven people avoided direct interference with the "other world" and were completely self sufficient. A significant difference was being made in the purification of the natural world. The earth was fighting to come back, with the people of N.O.T.R. acting like white blood cells in a giant body, healing multiple infections. The virus was an over abundance of red cells that no longer carried oxygen to the earth's brain or body, and created clogging. The Raven people knew the body would someday become immune to this virus, and kill it off. If it didn't, the people would die fighting, never stopping to destroy it. With no poison there would be healthy blood able to repair and restore the damage done. Rather, healthy people in a lively, balanced, natural world.

Cara was to help in this fight. She had abundant knowledge, passion in her soul and power in her flesh to lead in this fight. From the time spent in the cave or lost in space, Cara Sedalia was older now, an adult in the skin. It was obvious to her, why she was taken from her own time, and gifted with seeming super-human senses. She was here to heal the earth, understand it, and help rid it of this spreading virus. She had discovered her destiny.

No more pillaging, raping or bleeding of the land. She felt the earth's pain as if it were her own. It was deadly. She felt it like acid in the pit of her stomach. This was to become her battle, and the Tiger had equipped her so she would be ready. It was never stated when, but someday the time would come. First she would have to understand the earth, and live a new life.

After her time inside the cave with the god-like guidance of the white tiger, Cara was ready. She was to start from scratch, with no more than the clothes on her back and the wisdom in her brain. Things would fall into place as they always do, and Cara would know where to go when the time came. She was fully prepared. Or she had been, coming out of the cave, until she found the wolf pup.

Turning around, Cara looked for the pup's mother. There was nothing but open alpine hills,so the pup was alone. She called for the Tiger, and there was no response. The cave had dissapeared and so it seemed that Cara was alone too. Hesitating, she picked up the whimpering pup and cradled him like a baby child. There were no bites or resistance from the wolf pup, he gladly burrowed inside her jacket, happy to feel another body.
"I'll name you Risk, little wolfling."

Feeling like a child again, where everything is spectacular and new, Cara began to sing as she trudged through snow in search of a town.

Two

~~~~~~~~~~~~~~~~~~~~~~~

After a walk through a world of white hills and skies, a series of houses came into view. It was a town, population no more than 500. As Cara trudged through town, she heard dogs begin to bark and yowl, welcoming her. A man stepped outside of the second house on the right, where the yapping was coming from. He studied Cara briefly, and then decided she was of no threat. Changing his stature, he raised his voice to an audible, "Hello!" and he waved her to come in.

Inside, Cara was able to study the features of the man. He was tall, appearing to be around 50 years of age, and clothed in several layers of long johns. A stern face, worn and lived in, was sheltered by long, light gray strings of hair. Around him, the home was entirely made of wood. Small and cozy, the front door opened into a kitchen and den, with a stairwell to the side.

A fire burned in a pit, the center of the wooden living area. The man graciously welcomed her in, though he seemed shocked to have such a guest. It was then that Cara became aware of her new body. She had not yet seen her face, but from the moment she stepped inside the cabin, she realized she was a grown woman, and perhaps somewhat attractive. Little did she know that she was a striking 5'9" Native beauty with long dark hair, tan skin, doe eyes and round facial features.

The haggard home owner introduced himself as Ol' Jack Harrington, the leader of his town. Out back he had three dozen sled dogs that provided the town with reliable trade and transportation services. After finishing his introduction, Ol' Jack excused himself to hush the dogs and warm some milk on the stove. It was then that Cara removed Risk from inside her jacket, placing him on the wooden floor beneath her. Risk yawned and showed off the nubs of his puppy teeth. After giving Cara a warm lick on her fingers, he curled up and resumed his slumber.

While her host occupied himself in the kitchen, Cara heard the howling of wolves somewhere nearby. Ol' Jack stomped out of the kitchen, muttering that those "damn wolves from hell are back." as he set down two mugs of warm milk. He smiled briefly, revealing a missing front tooth and smugly told Cara if he ever saw another wolf again, he would slaughter it on the spot. It was then he noticed the wolf pup sitting beneath the feet of his guest. He raised a brow and his pulse began to increase. The hazel eyed mistress was very beautiful, with looks that could probably get her whatever she wanted from him. Jack kicked himself for the thought. A grudge was still a grudge, he reminded himself.

Cutting off his next train of thought, Cara explained that the pup beneath her was no more than a lost sled dog pup she found wandering outside his village. The man was in no mood to argue, and he let it go with a chiding remark of "yeah, well, we'll see." Cara smiled with all the charm she could manage. It brought a blush to Ol' Mr. Harrington's cheeks and he had to look away. The conversation was over.

Inside the house the two spoke for many hours, trading tales of adventure and fantasy. Cara was to speak nothing of her strange journey to this new age. Not of the glory of the Tiger, of her plans to rise in the new world, or her love for the wolf beneath her. Instead, Cara began weaving up an imaginary past. She said she had lost her relatives at an early age, and spent her years going from town to town in search of family. The story led up to the very moment at hand. It seemed to work well.

After being fully satisfied with Cara's explanation for appearing so suddenly, Ol' Jack told her his story. He was a man fond of the land, though weary of the wolves at his backdoor. They harassed his dogs, he claimed. On occasion they'd get hungry enough to pick the weakest as a snack. He had been wed to an ogre of a woman who passed away years before. Ol' Jack showed no remorse for his loss, claiming the woman had made his life a living hell, which had frozen over. Ol' Jack roared with a husky laughter from his joke. Cara caught the source of his amusement and doubled his sound. It felt good to laugh. After contentment was left echoing off the walls, the lines on Jack's forehead deepened, as he began another tale.

Truth or fiction, Ol' Jack said he had lost his two sons in a blizzard a year back. They had been working for an unnamable source far out in the woods. Years before his loss, Jack had held a private meeting with the foreign man from out of town. He simply requested that Harrington's sled dog pups be delivered to his home land every year. It was to be in exchange for his finest foals every spring season. The man explained his reclusive people were not to be imposed upon, and had bred the horses to gladly perform in the freezing temperatures. Though the horses did good work, his people desired dogs as well. It was to be a fair trade.

The man showed obvious signs of dislike for Jack Harrington, but would gladly allow Jack's oldest son, the man least like his father, the privilege of knowing their location. Jack never understood why he chose Bill. Before departing, the trader explained Bill would be the only one capable of access. Jack Harrington agreed, for such a strong breed of horse was plenty appealing. After smoking the pipe together, the deal was sealed, and it became so.

Bill always led the way up the pass, with his brother's sled of cargo close behind. Bill would always force his younger brother Chuck home a day early, allowing him to go the rest of the way alone. Chuck would never argue with his older brother. He was quiet and never said much, unless he had a reason.

No one in the village knew of the trading tribe's location. Town members would search for days in every direction, and find no traces of human civilization. Harrington's people gave up and considered the horse people gypsies. Bill never told anyone what their camp was like, or how he managed to find them. All the time, Bill never mentioned that he was the only human in their society who *could* even get there.

The third year the boys were making the special delivery, it had become a bit of a routine. The sixth day of the journey, Bill and Chuck were at the place where they often split; the beginning of an old evergreen forest, just beneath a mighty mountain. Bill gave Chuck a letter to take home to their father. Enclosed was a message that said in bold block print,

"I AM NOT COMING HOME. GOODBYE AND KEEP WARM." He never explained, just smiled and sent his brother home with his love. He also warned Chuck not to open the letter until he had returned home. After turning away from his brother, Chuck disobeyed and read the letter. He headed home with an empty sled and a heart full of sadness.

On the journey back to town, a fierce blizzard blew him and his team off course. They were not discovered until the thaw of the coming spring, two hundred miles outside of town. When they found Chuck's corpse frozen in a block of ice, they found the letter gripped in his hand. It was the first time any member of the clan had seen Jack Harrington cry.

After a moment's pause, Jack went on explaining how for the last few years various members from town had been lending their services to help with the dogs and community services. With all the rotating faces, the dogs never had one particular leader. They had begun acting poorly, some even depressed. Sorrow crossed Ol' Jack's face as he stood up, his back to Cara, facing the fire pit. As if he was drawing his words from the flames. He gazed deep into them until he collected his thought. After seeing his dialogue flicker from the flames, he quickly began to speak.

"You can care for these dogs better than any man in this town. I can sense it. Am I wrong Cara? You have walked into my house with a wild wolf in your arms, and yet he sleeps at your feet like a tame pet."

Cara took instant offense to the old man's reference to Risk as a pet. She was stunned he had admitted him to be a wolf. She studied Jack as he drew more words.

"Listen, you take care of these dogs and I will take care of you. There's my sons' empty room upstairs, take it. This house is warm, and I have enough food to feed two families. And now, that's more than most can say around these parts. Your company has warmed my heart, and I'd gladly see more of you here. The middle of winter is a quiet time, but we're real busy here. You'll have fun. Why, my town is nice, and you can stay as long as you like."

Jack pulled out the pipe from his stories. The pipe he smoked with the horse man. He was offering it to her.

"What'd' yaw say missy?"

She knew it at that very moment. This was what she would do. She wasn't entirely sure why, but she felt there was some hidden reason why it all felt so right. Meanwhile beneath her, Risk raised a sleepy brow and studied her face. It was as if he understood every word that had been said. Jack turned to Cara and he too, waited for her response.

"Alright."

That was all she said. A warm smile grew across her face and she inhaled from the magic green pipe. This action spoke to her host better than any words she could muster. This just seemed to make sense. It seemed perfect and right.

It would give her a chance to grow up with Risk, and adjust to the new world. Something made her believe that Risk was more than just some wolf pup. Surely there was a reason he was brought here too. Time would reveal all, she knew. It always does.

After another hour in the den smoking, Jack excused himself to bed. Risk followed the old man and fumbled up the wooden staircase. Giggling, Cara followed the floppy pup's lead. No more was to be said for now. After having a lengthy sleep in her new home, the Harrington cabin, Cara awoke to day one of her new life. Learning everyday, the months flew by like the golden eagles that soared above.

****

Working for Jack was not easy. He had quite the temper, and rarely stood for Cara's mistakes. Easily, she prevailed, learning from her errors and flourishing into success. Business was strong and she had formed a quality bond with each dog she cared for. The sled team was doing exceptionally well with her as their new leader. For the dogs, life was good. For her, life had finally gotten better.

Cara made runs for Jack and the town every week or so, alternating her crew of canine companions to avoid exhaustion of the dogs. Many trips were weeks long and, weather was often trying. The feeling of coming home from a lengthy journey left Cara with a burning high, and she was becoming addicted to the rush. She loved it. Especially when medicine was the delivery and lives were at ease because of the team's speedy arrival. Her dogs were her best friends. She felt their love, and at last, Cara was happy to just be.

With each day, Risk was growing strong and wise. He often spent his nights curled up at Cara's feet, or running with her through the depths of the forest. Every night she was home, he was by her side. Risk was too young to pull with the big dogs when they left to make a run. The times Cara left Risk home, Jack enlisted his talents and put him to work mushing and towing smaller amounts of weight. Harrington would harness him up to a wheelbarrow, or an old tire, and let him pull until the night came on. Every day he was kept busy and challenged.

Time had begun to prove to Cara that there was much more to Risk than big paws and a happy smile. He had begun to communicate with her, in a way she was familiar with. The way he spoke was like the way the trees called her name. I reminded her of her ever-fading past. The wolfing spoke directly to her, and she understood his every thought. One night she realized, camping out in the thawing woods of Canada, Risk could hear and understand her, as well.

It was the beginning of their second spring on the north western slopes of Canada. They were returning from another lengthy trip, silently running in the hazy dusk, Cara's skin was pimpled with chills. Somewhere in the forest, she heard the singing of the wolves. There was joy in the howls and it sounded like three adults. The echoed one another and crooned to the perfect song.

The team was a day out of town and the dogs were showing signs of tiring. They were worn out. They'd managed to get too cold and too hungry to run much farther into the night. As they loped over another mile, Cara began scouting out a safe pocket of forest to find rest and shelter.

Another beckoning call wafted across the still night air. Cara knew the wolves would come down to the valley to follow the herds of elk, moose, and caribou that found sanctuary in the generous meadows. It was all part of the great migration, and it was beautiful. In turn, it was Ol' Jack's sled team that often had to face the consequences of being in the wrong place during the wrong season.

Cara had offered the idea of moving locations for the first part of spring, allowing the wolves to pass through the valley without the temptation of "doggie snacks". Often enough, when the wolves passed through, members of the team became stir crazy and would escape from their pens to chase the call of the wild. Some dogs were never seen again and thought to have joined the wolves' pack. However it was more likely that the carcass of the dog would be found, brutally massacred from a wolf fight.

Despite multiple attempts on Cara's behalf, the man was as stubborn as an ox, and would have none of her ideas of dog relocation. He thought it was a form of giving in to the wolves. Letting them win some imaginary battle he refused to explain. As the wolves echoed the slopes again, Cara said aloud,

"Stay out of town to stay alive!"

After unhooking the dogs from their harnesses, Cara

pulled out her thermal blanket from the side of the sled, and curled up beneath it. Camp was set up, the dogs were fed and it was time to rest. She was exhausted, no doubt about it. She'd close her eyes and wait for sleep to come but the howling of the wolves managed to keep her up. Most of her dogs were asleep, cuddly little balls of colored fur. Their bushy tails shielded the soft, tender flesh of their noses from the elements.

Deep breathing alongside her back accompanied the warmth of another body pressed against her. Queen, the team's bulkiest female had backed herself up against her favorite human. The only wolf on the team, she shared a very special bond with Cara. Thinking about that made her smile. Queen often acted as a mother to Risk when they first arrived. When he was very young, Queen would tend to him when they were on the road, keeping him warm and guarding him from aggressive team members. At the Harrington place, she would keep Risk company, and try to show him the wild ways of the wolf.

Cara closed her eyes and listened. There was absolute silence other than the occasional dripping of snow from the branches of the towering trees. Her mind was working overtime and letting her know it. She flip-flopped under her blankets. Internally, she was fidgeting.

There was something more to the wolf songs. The wolves were getting closer instead of going south, into the town. She sighed and let her warm breath curl into the cold air. It had to be something about their calls. They sounded as if they were searching rather than hunting for something. Maybe they had lost someone. After a few more minutes, Cara managed to shrug it off. A deep sleep eagerly consumed her body and swallowed her brain into silence.

Cued by Cara's sound sleep, Risk tensed. Breathing deep, he stood up and began sniffing the wind. He was trying to locate his brethren, to lead them to the end of their search. He glanced at his sleeping friends, then out into the darkness. Trotting off into the wind, Risk looked back once more to witness puffs of fog rising from Cara's sleeping spot. It was very cold for a human. He was glad she was used to it and did not seem to suffer.

The dropping temperatures made Risk's bones feel hollow, allowing the cold to echo through his limbs as he stood. His body resisted. It craved the warmth and comfort sleep could provide. But he shook it off, and burst into a sprint to gain as much distance from the dogs as he could. He needed to respond to the wolves' call and give them their location before they gave up and changed directions.

He'd managed to kick off his protective booties and the chill sliced like a knife in between his foot pads as he ran. His body shook like a plastic case around him. It had become so cold that he feared his bones might snap in half. He could imagine them shattering like a pane of glass, but the animal instinct overcame his increasingly human imagination. Wolf spirit made him numb to the pain as he continued to gain distance from camp.

After a half a mile was between him and the team, he let out a lengthy howl. It quivered as he began; nerves and lack of practice gave his youth away in an instant. He let the sound go on, trying with each tone change to steady his sound. In response, a hush fell over the night. Risk stood there listening, in wait. He began to pace in anticipation and impatience.

He called again. This time, the howl that erupted from his throat awakened a nesting bald eagle in the tree above. The eagle's eyes widened in an attempt to soak up the moon light and allow her to see where the noise that had startled her had come from. When she looked down and saw the young wolf beneath her, she saw that his sound had startled him as well. She clicked her beak in laughter at the wolf. There was no real threat and she tucked her beak back into her breast.

Less than a mile away, this time Risk heard an answer. The pack had narrowed in on his location and was bounding over the layers of snow to get to him. What Risk did not hear was the loping of sled dogs and the gliding of a sled behind them. Moments after the wolves' last call had been lost to the sky, they emerged from the forest.

All the commotion disturbed the eagle again and she watched them congregating under her tree. The same tree she returned to year after year to nest and raise her young. Fluffing her feathers inflated her shadowy figure to twice its massive size. She gave out a scornful caw to the rebels beneath her. The lead alpha bowed his head to the eagle, as if in apology. This wolf was old and wise, it showed through the way he seemed to walk with the earth, rather than trample its surfaces. He gazed at Risk warmly and then spoke to the two wolves at his side,

"Let's move. Risk, take me to your pack."

"Right."

Risk felt proud that the alpha had referred to the dogs as *his* pack. The three wolves followed his lead through the winding woods, until they arrived a hundred feet short of Cara and the team, all of whom were still asleep and warm. Risk wanted to know what this was all about. Why he had been chosen to guide these wolves to Cara, and if it was indeed for their benefit as Queen had promised.

With the clearing of the woods, only sparse trees scattered the terrain. It was brighter in the clearing and Risk was able to more clearly make out his company. The alpha wolf was a rich gray, shaggy and narrow-snouted. Rawhide was his name, and he had warm buttery eyes that were defined by a mask of black. The fur along his face was freckled with white and shades of smoke.

His pack was made up of a younger pair of males, each with markings resembling that of a German shepherd. Muted earth tones swirled together with darker patches and stripes of black. Their tails hung low, hugging the sides of their legs. There was no threat imposed by either of them for they were younger than he. The laws of canine dominance don't change; every member of the genus can always find their place.

Flashing white teeth in a grin, Rawhide studied the team of snoozing dogs. He focused on Cara and watched her breathing rhythmically. Her breath moved her sleeping bag up and down. Up and down, up and down. Watching Rawhide, Risk felt his hackles go up in defense mode. Body tensed, he was ready to spring at the slightest flinch from Rawhide.

Instead of an attack, Risk watched Rawhide's buttery eyes drift over and focus on something just past Cara. What was it he saw? Risk followed his stare. He was watching Queen, the only other wolf on the team. Sure Queen's father had a bit of mutt in him, but her looks and actions begged to differ. Why was he gazing at her? As if to answer his thought, Rawhide eased to his stomach and let out a quiet whimper. Queen's ears perked up, coming as a surprise to Risk. Even wolf ears would have had to strain to hear Rawhide's whine at such high frequency.

Still on all fours, alert and ready, Risk stood. He took a quick glance around to absorb his surroundings. Opposite him, the two young wolves were slouching in their stance. They seemed to be more interested in the smells of the night air than in the actions of their guide. Ears rotating, Risk picked up the typical sounds of the alpine eve. Not far off, he listened to the sound of another predator, sloughing through snow flour. Most likely, it was a badger nearby, out on the prowl of his territory. Or maybe he was chasing another, perhaps a mate. It seemed the dashes across the ground hit opposite the other, meaning more than one animal indeed. Either way, Risk lost his focus when he saw Queen from the corner of his eye stalking towards them.

Hackles went up again. Did she not see him? Were these wolves the wrong pack? Queen had delivered a message from a pack of wolves giving the details of this very night. All Risk knew was to do as he was instructed, trust Queen, and someday again, he would see that great White Tiger.

Because of the mighty spirit, Risk had been spared the slow death of a typical motherless wolf pup. His hunger was gone. His lice and the worms that had been tunneling his heart into a home were gone. Then there was Cara, a wolf in human flesh. She had taken care of him, nurtured him, and given him warmth that no furred animal could ever replace. Because of Cara, Risk understood love. He would pass it on, teach his seed to love. It is true that animal's can and do love. But like that of human's, love can be destroyed, lost and forgotten. Perhaps it was to be that Risk, the timber wolf had a mission of his own.

Meanwhile Rawhide began to squirm as Queen drew near. He put his tail up high and began wildly swishing it to and fro. He wagged so hard that his whole rear end was rocking from side to side, swiveling his hind paws into the layers of snow. Queen's stalking grew into a lope, her head still close to the ground as if she were on the hunt. She was giving mixed signals. Or maybe this was a bit of a game. Either way Risk was tense with anxiety to see the outcome of their actions. He wouldn't have to wait long, for her lope morphed into a silent bolt. Her mouth opened releasing her pink tongue, blown to one side measuring her increasing speed. Her ears were pressed to her skull and her eyes grew wide with excitement.

Queen stopped short just in front of swiveling Rawhide. She slapped her paws on the ground and stuck her tail in the air, mimicking Rawhide. He let out a few playful barks, allowing Queen to respond with a growling hum. As if an explosion went off between them, the two began chasing each other in circles. After a few laps, they promptly collapsed into each other and followed up their excursion with licking, nuzzling and head bowing. It was as if the two had been mates. After a few moments of the courting and introduction, it became clear as they piled atop each other. They *were* mates.

Rawhides' yearlings watched excitedly as their alpha passed on his growth to the hardy she-wolf. The romping that was slowly winding down woke Cara, and a few of the dogs. The awakened mutts erupted with ruffs and growls that were sure to wake the rest immediately.

She threw her sleeping bag off she secured each dog's harness to the sled. Cara worked fast. She could handle the wild in a minute but for now, Jack Harrington was in no shape to loose his dogs.

She was almost finished securing the final dog, Cara kept her eyes on the wolves. The five were sitting in a line waiting for her. She paused and noticed she was short two team members. Her wolves.

Standing tall Cara studied the five wolves. Quickly she was able to make out Queen and Risk, in the midst of the other three. They all just sat there, there was no fighting. They were just sitting there; the largest was relaxing on his haunches with ease. Grabbing her knife from its strap off the sleigh, Cara headed off towards the wolves.

As she approached, the dog's noise faded into the chill of the night air. Rather than continuing to wildly sound their excitement, the dogs turned somber. They were watching. The dogs became the audience for the confrontation of woman and wolf. They did not communicate emotions or thought with one another, they simply watched and waited. Waited, to break free and dash to their human's rescue.

It was like a scene from a movie Cara had once seen as she trudged through heavily packed snow, the wind ripping through her hair. Across from her, the wolves just sat and waited. It was as if they weren't fazed by the sudden gusts slicing across their shaggy hides. Glancing down only to check her footing, she thought of how to act upon this scene; three strange wolves sitting in a row. Next to, she mentally added, her closest friends. It was clear that a slow approach would be best. And it would buy her time to continue assessing the situation.

Staring down the line of lupus lupus, Cara first noted the contentment Queen showed. Knowing that she too was wild inside, Cara was not entirely surprised when she noticed her leaning against the outsider. Queen was comfortably close to the largest wolf of the three. He was dark gray and has a scruffy appearance. Two younger wolves sat next to the larger one, obviously their alpha. They were young and awkwardly skinny. The yearling's eyes glowed with intrigue as Cara kept on towards them, plunging through the snow. At the opposite end of the line was Risk. He was next to Queen, nervously rocking as he waited for her. If he was with them, something was definitely up. What was this, a council? Cara couldn't help but wonder.

With an explosion of snow, Risk leaped up and dashed to greet her. The wolves scoffed at him but he could contain himself no longer. Ears low and tail wagging; Cara passed her knife to her left hand and gave Risk an accepting pat on the head.

"What's goin' on here, boy?"

Responding to Cara's call for Risk, the large shaggy wolf approached Cara head on, giving Risk no time to respond. The foreign wolf's ears were up, but he left his tail in no particular position. It was just trailing behind him in neutral stance.

The shaggy wolf managed to stand in front of Cara as he had originally planned and glared Risk to her side. This way, he could look at them both, in the eyes, and be sure he faced no threats from behind. Satisfied with his positioning, he sat up tall, showed off his size and began to speak.

"I am Rawhide, the alpha of my pack. We come from a territory miles away. We're on an important mission all though I am sorry to have startled you. But you see, we were sent to this valley to find you and your wolf."

Cara's knife remained steady in her hand, with the blade appropriately angled. She was ready to cut his throat if his body language changed so much as a hair. He was too close to her for her to take any chances. Behind Rawhide, Queen remained still as a statue. She was listening, with a bit of a smile across her black wolfy lips. That prevented Cara from making any move prematurely. She would listen to Rawhide, and wait for any cues from Queen.

"Okay Rawhide..."

Cara trailed off, mesmerized by the gleaming of his presented fangs. He needed to close his mouth for her to concentrate better. She wasn't afraid of the wolf, but his size and poise was a bit distracting. That and, he said he was sent searching for her. Hopefully he was not sent on a search and destroy mission, she would hate to disappoint him. That thought filled her with self-assurance, and when she began to speak this time, there was a tone of arrogance in her voice to him.

"Well who sent you strange wolf? And what is it you want with us? It's a little cold and dark for my lame senses to be accepting visitors, a threat on the other hand...I will respond to." Cara had no problem admitting her human handicap to the wolves. She often wondered if that would make her opponent underestimate her, and give her the opportunity to kill and win.

"A challenge already? I recall the warning about you, girl. Just listen. There is another human nearby. He is the one you must meet. He holds information that you require. I honestly know little of his intentions but can guarantee you no harm. This arrangement is from the Spirit lands, so you may lower your hand-fang there."

Cara glanced at her knife, a hand fang. She couldn't help but laugh. No doubt its pointy tip had become a bit of a threat to any animal who ever witnessed its deadly uses. She was still unsure of all this. She still had questions, so she deliberately ignored the alpha's request.

"What's Queen doing with you? Was she your pack? And why, Risk, did you go find them? You knew how the dogs would act."

Risk glanced up at Cara. His eyes were dark from his expanded pupil. He was drawing in all light to study her face.

"How did you know I left? There is no way you heard me. I was silent, and you were making the sounds of sleep."

Smiling down at her wolf, she briefly took in how handsome he was becoming. He was going to be very big someday; his massive paws deep in the snow were evidence of that. His body was evenly filling out and compared to the other wolf yearlings, he looked to be about full grown. But she knew better.

The color of his fur was made up of dimensions of grays and whites, fading to the color of dark stone at the tip of each hair. His fur was dazzling, marbled like a mountain. The swirls of color covered all of his body spare his paws, chest, cheeks and muzzle. They were left a milky white. It looked as if he wore socks, the way his fur changed so abruptly. The dark stripe down Risk's muzzle moved to the right, as his head turned to face Queen.

"Queen, come here and speak. Explain what you know and why I am here now."

There was a tone of authority in his request. He was a potentially powerful male, despite his lack of experience. None the less, Queen obeyed as if he were alpha himself, and she trotted over to them. Stopping only to lick Rawhide's snout, she then sat and gazing up at Cara with Rawhide at her side. Was this a face off?

"Cara, Rawhide is my mate and has been for the past twenty moons. I told him of your arrival when I first learned of you. You see, Rawhide's territory is far away and only reachable if one journeys across a very sacred path. It can only be traveled by certain creatures. I believe the people refer to us as animal royalty, can you believe that? I was born from that place and abandoned here by the man who employed Jack's sons. I used to follow his horses. But that's why I call myself Queen."

Rawhide snorted with impatience. Behind Cara, the sled dogs started up with whines and barks of interest and curiosity.

"It is my responsibility to take you to the other human. He has spent time in my country and is another who can walk the sacred path."

"Well, I'll follow you with the dogs. Risk can chase your scent without getting squeamish, so I'll put him up front. Let's go guys; I'm getting frozen out here!"

Queen made off towards the sled while Risk remained close to Cara's side. Rawhide spoke once more,

"He is not too far. I believe he set up fire, to keep warm in wait. Hopefully that will be motivation to your dogs as well as your wolf."

He eyed Risk sternly, but he did not cower from his gaze. With a swish of a tail, Rawhide took off. His two yearlings sprinted behind Rawhide, hurling their bodies forward to gain enough speed. Within minutes, they disappeared just as suddenly as they had arrived. Now they were gone, ghosts dashing through the woods.

Cara was silent as she and Risk ran back to the sled. Neither knew what to expect next but neither wanted to loose the wolves up ahead. Queen was hooked up to the right side rear of the pack, as usual. In front was Risk for the first time. The team of dogs didn't protest once Cara headed back to the sled. Even the lead dog, Heron, was too enthralled to challenge Risk. He watched Risk's yellow eyes glow with eagerness and passion. He was rather glad that the two had not yet been in quarrel for leadership. There was no longer a competition. Heron licked the frost of his own nose and admitted he was fully thrilled to follow the wolf's lead.

"MUSH!"

Cara's command was the cue Risk was waiting for. Pointing his body towards the woods he gave a short howl to inform the team of their destination. Leaping forward he stumbled briefly from expecting the weight of the team to be on his shoulders. Each dog distributed the load so that for the lead, there was little weight to carry and only speed to gain. Regaining his footing, he gracefully plowed through the snow with ease. The other dogs, including Heron, didn't seem to notice his misstep. Risk's senses were alert and performing at their peak despite the hunger and cold. The events throughout the evening had kept his blood pumping hot.

Entering the forest, Queen was completely pleased with Risk, Cara, Rawhide and herself. All in all, she was pleased with all the magic in her life.

Through everything she had ever seen in all her wolfy years, the moment around her, the sight before her, made for a truly mystical moment. Things had gone just as she had hoped they would from the time she met Risk to the moment she heard him take off to answer Rawhide's calls. Inside her belly, her beloved mate's seed was planted and the future pups would have a mission of all their own.

As she pulled, she kept her eyes on Risk's swishing tail up in front. He paced his breathing and lolled his tongue out in ecstasy. He was every bit a leader, to wolf and dog. Queen echoed Risk's call, howling in meaningless communication. Though she knew what was in store once they reached the man in the woods, she said nothing. She was still young enough to thrive on surprises.

Racing past the toes of the tall, tall trees, Risk feared he had lost his scent. Rawhide's trail had been gone for a distance, replaced by the prints of forest creatures astir in the oncoming spring dawn. Risk was searching for signs of a wolf's recent travel. With the pressure intensifying as each breath processed through his body, so much as a trampled patch of forest floor could turn his direction, but there was nothing. He barked a stop to the dogs and they obeyed. Cara didn't step off her pegs to check on Risk, she knew that he was the only one who would lead them to the wolves. So all she did was shiver and wait.

Risk hushed his rapid breath and pointed his ears in every direction. He heard nothing more than the wet, sloppy snow plopping off branches and the hum of life in the forest. No animal other than a rodent nearby, stirred enough to make a sound. Risk opened his mouth and licked his nose. He tried to taste the air and smell any fraction of scent that could guide him to the end of his challenge. Rawhide was skilled and his trail was clean.

Bowing down, his weight resting on his elbows, Risk lowered his head to the ground. He felt the pulse of running not too far away. A map was being drawn inside his head, guiding him to the sound. Risk lifted his head in another howl, calling to Rawhide, letting him know he found his trail and was on the way. Cara cracked her whip on the side of the team to bring their attention to the moment. Behind Risk, Heron had been listening to the ground in attempt to hear what Risk heard. He heard nothing. Risk was going on pure instinct, without a doubt. Whatever he had heard was only his heart taking charge and putting him on the move. After so many years in the lead, Heron knew that the mind could play tricks on a dog. Was the frost making a fool of the wolf as well?

Running was intense. Exhaustion was turning the younger dogs delirious. They would have bursts of speed powered by the fear of a shadow cast or of a stone kicked up that nicked at their heels. They were becoming disorganized and slowing the entire team down. Cara yelled out commands accordingly but knew that their cowardice was her fault. Still she made them press on.

At last, Risk's instinct led them all to the Promised Land. A dip in the land scattered with sparse trees. In the centermost point of the circle, a raging fire burned tall to the cloudless sky. The sun was beginning to peak over the mountains and hills, painting all the earth a violet hue.

Risk stood in silence and awaited a command to come from either Cara or his gut. Shaking from the emptiness of her stomach, Cara stepped off the pegs of the sled to stand on her own. She waited for her head to clear and form an idea.

In front of her were a similar sled, four dogs, and one ball of human under a sleeping bag. Both the man and the dogs were soundly asleep. Cara panned her view back and forth, trying to find the wolves that lead Risk here. Did he take her to the wrong man? Surely that was too much of a coincidence to be the case. She couldn't help but wonder. Stepping to the front harness, Cara unhooked Risk and knelt down to give him a rough pat on his side.

"You did a good job Risk. Now go find the wolves without waking these others. We'll wait here."

Risk didn't argue for he knew Cara could take the man if he dare threatened her. And his team mates, as much as they refused their wolf heritage, were wilder than any other team Risk had ever seen. Also they out-numbered the man's four by six of their own. Finishing his thoughts, Risk shook loose the ice crystals that had matted to his fur. Glancing once more around him, he gave a snort to Cara, and took off alone.

She watched as Risk disappeared into the distance. She quaked from the reminder of her own body's discomfort. Looking to the team, she saw that the dogs looked like a haggard bunch. Most stared at an invisible target with their eyes drooping. Some were hunched over. Others were leaning against each other to steal a moment of sleep. Dragging Risk's empty harness behind her, Cara walked down the small slope to the level center of the dip. The dogs and the sleigh followed behind her.

The flop of the sled didn't wake the man below. Instead he curled up into a tighter ball, hugging the warmth of his sleeping bag. A few of his dogs twitched their ears, but none rose to greet her. The consistent snaps and crackles of the glowing fire camouflaged the noise Cara made as she unhooked her dogs from their harnesses. Free from the sled they looked at Cara, debating which urge was greater, sleep or hunger.

She had to feed them all, she knew that their stomachs were as empty as hers. A moment of animal instinct overruled her human use of routine and schedule. If she brought out the food, the aroma would stir the sleeping dogs and potentially attract predators. Deciding on a plan, Cara patted each canine member down. She checked for injury and whispered them to sleep. Rather than dining in the warming frost of the dawn, the dogs curled up amongst one another and immediately fell asleep. Their motionless resting was a sign to Cara. The sign of the *right* choice.

Though the comfort and warmth the sleeping bag was swallowing her in, Cara was reluctant to rest. Her eyes grew heavy as cinder blocks, yet she forced them open. She watched the towering forest walls around her for any sign of anything. Just as her eyelids gave up and closed, Risk came to lick her cheek. She awoke gently to him. Not in shock or defense as she often did to others. Rising, she yawned and dug her fingers deep into Risk's coat. She whispered into the pink of his ear,

"Where are the wolves?"

Risk replied,

"I found them feeding on an old kill, not to far from here. They told me that this dip in the land is a cradle to all creatures who seek refuge between the trees. A yearling said there was a sleeping spell cast here that doesn't allow one to rise until his health and vitality is restored. And I believe him! I mean, look! I'm quiet but still... there should be animals stirring!"

Cara curved her lips in amusement.

"I know Risk, I believe it too. So what happens next? Are we all to sleep into the high sun of the day?"

"Yes, that human male and those dogs share our exhaustion. Rawhide said those dogs have also traveled many a mile and they will wake up only after we are all fully alert."

"Okay... and when will we be seeing that wolf again? Or was all this some kind of scam to delay my progress on the trail?"

"I don't think the spirits would scam us, Cara I'm sure they have better things to do."

"So you think they're strictly working for greater purposes at all times? No way! They get bord just like we do. Besides, you're delirious."

Risk growled deep in his throat. If Cara's hands were not in his ruff, she wouldn't have known it. She smirked at him, mockingly showing her own fangs. He understood the gesture.

"Rawhide and his pack said they'd be here when we get up. Then I imagine the meeting will begin, or whatever is supposed to happen next. Whatever it is must be very important 'cause I can feel it like a weight inside my stomach."

"That weight is usually a sign of something big. You're right and you've been sounding very wise today Risk. I'm proud of you, pup." Risk twitched his ear, as if he hadn't heard this at all. He hated being so young, his age was his handicap. He looked down and then nipped at the base of Cara's chin. She chuckled quietly at his silly little games.

Together they lay down to rest. Risk tucked his tail over his nose and closed his yellow eyes to rest under Cara's arm and blanket. No matter where he had ever been, Risk always felt safe and at home curled up with Cara. Her warm breath would slow, and pulse against his skin. Her face was warm and her skin was soft, often buried in the ruff of his neck. This was where he belonged. She needed him to get by, and he needed her in return. Stress melted away and he fell into a deep state of sleep beside the living thing he cared deeply about.

Three
~~~~~~~~~~~~~~~~~~~~~~

The forest remained still as the sun came up and swallowed the grays of dawn. The singing and chirping of the morning birds was light. They were cooing a wispy lullaby it seemed, and their voices only aided Cara and the dog's sleep. The large man across the fire kept his face hidden but quaking snores rose in the mid-day heat.

At noon, the sun sat perched atop thick clouds that streaked the sky. It was at its tallest position, and Cara began to wake up. Before opening her eyes she tensed and listened. The fire was silent in its death, and she was able to hear the yawns of her dogs as they too began to rise. Crawling out of her sleeping bag, she rolled it up and set it aside. Cara could hear the snow beneath her cringe as it packed itself together beneath her feet.

Things on the other side of the fire were still. It seemed the company was still asleep. Above them, the three wolves had arrived and were standing at attention. As if greeting a human friend, Cara waved to them. It was moments like this in the isolated wilderness that she felt embarrassed about her habit of greeting another with this pointless gesture. When she came across others and waved, they often went into a panic or she simply scared them away.

The wolves did not turn and leave. Instead Rawhide slid his paws forward, sending his belly to the ground and his legs to the side. The yearlings copied their alpha, each stretching out to a lounging pose. It was comical. So much for the scheme, Cara thought.

She proceeded to pack away her blankets and bring out the food stash. The supply was almost gone, for the team was not far from home. Cara hated carrying extra weight but it was times like these that made her wish she would listen to others more often and carry more with her. She wished to have something to offer to her host. A bag of kibbles stirred with corn was the meal she provided for her dogs. The meat she had taken was gone, but pieces of jerky and dried fish partially made up the kibbles. She had something else in mind for her morning meal.

Fry bread. Sweet, salty, and thin. Cara ate it ravenously, as if to imitate her team's feasting manners. The fire had been brought back to its former glory when Cara turned around from finding her food and she planned to take full advantage of the heat. As she finished the last bites of her meal, she gave her dogs boiled snow water to drink. She then quenched her own thirst with the crisp, cool water.

Across the flames, the man was sitting on top of his sled. He was thick, heavy-looking and big. She imagined he could snap her spine like a straw. She often did not see this possibility in the strangers she met. That she thought of this from him was thrilling.

Cara waited for him to jolt up and attack but the handsome stranger did not move.

Beneath him, his own dogs gobbled up kibble and he ripped off a hunk of tough venison with his teeth and chewed. His jaw muscles flexed with a strength that could probably crush bones. Watching from the corner of her eye, she finished swallowing. He waited for her to set down her canteen before he stood to approach her. He walked a few paces, and then stopped at the fire pit. He was waiting before crossing to her side of the circle. Knife in hand and Risk at her back, she walked to meet the bear of a man face to face.

He was a good five inches taller than she, and far wider. He was a large man but had the definition of a sculpture. He seemed to be endless pounds of pure muscle. His skin was a light tan color, a shade darker than hers. He had few wrinkles in his face for he was still young. Those that did exist were cracks from sun and years of smiling and laughter. Looking into his eyes, Cara felt warmth exude from his soul. It made his amber eyes twinkle like those of a young child at play. Cara tensed as he raised a hand to his heart, for it reminded her of the paw of a grizzly.

As his hand lay atop his heart, eyes locked with hers, Cara returned his greeting. She put her hand in the center of her chest, and extended her arm forward, palm up. Watching her do so, the man took his hand off his chest and held his arm out as well completing the peace greeting. This action, she had quickly learned, replaced the handshake of her distant old world. He was offering her access to his core.

This gesture's meaning was so simple and pure. It was often used to communicate with what Cara learned to call "beast people", were-people, skin walkers, shape shifters. At times she wondered if she was one of them.

The hand atop the heart was to signify the meeting place of the heart, soul, and mind. The place where emotions, thoughts and feelings came from. If the person tapped their hand on their chest, it meant that they did not wish to open up and communicate. Sometimes one would beat on his chest with force to scare away his questioner. When that was the case, the greeting would be over and each member moved on. It is not rude, but it allows people to be safe in their own minds, and others safe *from* their minds.

However if the hand extends out, it means the person will give their thoughts to the other, and they wish to communicate. The time of a living creature is a gift, but should never be forced. It is said by Raven medicine women that a shifter may need the time to grow familiar with the shapes of human words. Cara had never met a shifter, but the gentleness in this stranger made her dismiss any fantasies of meeting one now. So she returned his gesture, tucked her knife away and waited for him to speak.

"I am Whispering Bill."

A steady voice with a gentle tone came out of the man's mouth. He had the accent of the old-world Cherokee warriors. Such speech was often wise and simple while being blunt and commanding. Cara swallowed her swoon and nodded, cueing him to continue speaking. There was a long pause. She waited, but he did not speak.

Standing nose to nose, they were close enough to be lovers but their eyes were locked as they studied each other. Bill seemed fascinated by her. It seemed to have been a long while sense he last viewed another of his kind. To Cara, Bill smiled and the warmth from his soul oozed out like the sap of a growing maple tree.

She was dumbfounded. His name sounded so familiar, as if it could roll off her tongue with the ease of her own.....*Whispering Bill*. Sigh. Perhaps the man had mistaken her for someone else. Presenting himself before her, the way he showered warmth onto her was like that of a family member or a long loved pack mate. It was just unusual but then again, so was she.

"Um, hi. I'm uh, Sedalia. It is nice to meet you." Smooth, real smooth, she thought. She laughed at herself and pressed herself to continue.

" See, the wolves brought me to you, saying you needed me." Cara couldn't help but blush at the bluntness of her statement.

"Do you have your persons confused? I don't remember ever meeting you but you..."

Her words trailed off, only to have Whispering Bill pick them back up and finish her sentence.

"You never have met me, but you have worked for my father now for quite some time. I know about the wolves and I know about you, Cara. I-"

"You are the lost boy Bill!?"

"I was hardly a boy then and even less of one now. And aren't we all lost on this earth? At least I am not confused."

"Well neither am I but where have you been? Where did you go to? I'm sorry, I've always wondered and-"

"And you will find out shortly. Tell me, why did you not give me your first name? It's obvious you are female. I mean, giving me your last name hides nothing."

Cara flashed a scowl to Bill, for she had so much she wanted to say to him. She didn't expect him to be so inquisitive of her. She wanted to tell him how she had always used him as a bit of a role model back at the cabin, a standard for her own greatness with Jack Harrington and the team. She wanted to be better than him, or at least as great as he, in her own way. Now with his identity revealed, Cara felt both impressed and empowered in his presence.

The things she did *not* want to tell him was how when her mind drifted at night, she often imagined how the mysterious young man ran off to some feral world, waiting for her. Somewhere he could be free of rules, the ever watching eyes of the small village, the stress from his favored younger brother and his governing father, forever. She wanted to believe that he was like her.

Often Cara would think of a place lush and green in the summer months where he stayed, A place with roaming bears, wolves, moose, geese and caribou. Maybe he could even speak with them, as she did with the wild animals of the forests. Although the dogs were harder to speak with, mind to mind, but that was of little importance in this case.

On especially cold nights, Cara would even dream of Whispering Bill, imagining him to be just as handsome and strong as the character standing before her. She was old enough to understand love and often wished it would come and find her. Maybe take her away into another world that had a place for her and Whispering Bill to be together, and together they would stay. She dreamt up a bit of every woman's fantasy, no matter her age.

Back to the conversation, Cara focused and remembered she needed a witty retort.

"Well I guess I...I don't know. My name is Cara Sedalia. Cara, Bill.... Better?" Her tartness seemed to sting him and it looked like it hurt. She hoped it did not anger him as her feistiness did his father. It seemed his lips twitched, almost cracking a smile. That was a good sign.

"Cara. Okay. You let me explain things first."

Bill explained his disappearance to Cara. The details of his story hardly differed from those of Cara's fantasy tale. Indeed he was fed up with the ways of his father and was not the son favored by him. His younger brother Chuck was the image of their father. That bonded the two even closer and cast a shadow over Bill throughout his life. Nothing he did was ever good enough for Jack, not even the way he looked.

Bill captured the looks of his birth mother, a different woman than his brother's mother, his father's wife. His mother had died during childbirth and was not often spoken of. Chuck's mother was never attached to Bill and without a mother's love, he cried at night. He felt so alone. The only casual mentioning of her was that of her free spirit and love of wild horses.

He learned that his mother was a gypsy woman, wild and striking as the lands she roamed. She spent her summers in the mountains and hills, finding shelter in the village during the winters. She sold goods to the people in exchange for their hospitality and services. Each year she would be followed by a small herd of horses. When leaving in the spring, she would give the village a foal from her finest white mare. It would always prove to be the most reliable steed in town.

The woman was full of laughter and happiness. Her joy seemed to be the cure Jack Harrington needed to aid his trampled soul. The local woman he had been courting was caught in bed with a traveling man, and it did his heart no good to see her happiness with him. Jack's heart had been broken for he was not as impressive to the girl. Jack, at the time, did not understand why he should be less to her. He worked hard, built a good home and would make a fine husband. Yet she married the other man, running off with him to another country. She left Jack cold and alone, until he noticed the beauty of the gypsy.

Year after year Jack Harrington continued to be intrigued and enchanted by the woman's visits. She was sweet and made the village people smile. Her knowledge and respect of animals matched his own and he felt they shared more than that in common. Young Harrington would often care for the foals she left with the town, their progress was something that bonded her to him and he liked that. Every moment of every day Jack thought of nothing but ways to get closer to the wild angel of his dreams.

The gypsy came to stay in the village as the final leaves fell from the deciduous trees of the forest. She did not come into town on horseback however, as she always had. This time she rode in a sled led by ten large dogs. Behind her was the herd of horses led by the noble white mare, as usual. She stayed though the winter and on to the spring, singing songs to the people and telling tales of the spirit world that she knew. She told the children that that was where she came from along with her magnificent white mare.

Meanwhile Jack Harrington was becoming favored by the village people as a chief. He was a born leader, sharp, stern, fair and wise. It came to be that he was the chosen one to govern the village in the years to come. Until that day, Jack passed the time caring for the woman's animals, along with his own. He didn't like to show it, but Mr. Harrington was a very compassionate man, though his deception did not fool the gypsy. The woman smiled upon him and adored his dedication to practice and repetition.

The way he lived his life seemed to be a style she could never have. He was the opposite of her: grounded, consistent, steady. She took pride in what she was: an ever changing drifter, a dreamer. It only made sense to her for the two to merge. So one spring night after strong wine and fine weather with Jack, she told him how she felt he completed her and made her whole. He gave her his heart that night, swearing its trueness even after death. That night, they bonded deeply and created life from their endless love.

With a child growing inside of her, the gypsy took a year off from travel. The village let her horses into their barns and made her feel quite cozy and at home. They did not know, until it showed, of the child that was soon to come. Jack was ecstatic from her company; he never wanted her to leave his side. He wanted marriage from the woman and it pained her to tell him it was something she could never provide. She had made her plans; rather the spirits had made them for her. She would give birth to their child and then take him with her to the land given to the strong of heart and soul. The child would be able to walk both worlds as she did.

~~~~~~

The seasons Jack Harrington spent with the horse woman were the happiest times of Mr. Harrington's life. He too was whole, full in his heart. It was a feeling that terrified him and thrilled him all the same. He was no longer in control of his life or his emotions. They all belonged to *her*. What she did with them, he did not care. His heart was hers. The softest part of his being was in the hands of another and he loved it.

Jack's mate was never tamed; she would leave to wander the woods without notice. He could do nothing but let her go, praying that she would always return to him. Often she would ride her horses out on long journeys, some of which Jack could simply not keep up with. Laughing she would reach the top of the mountain and wait for him to arrive. She was always there for him. She was his and he hers. Finally, he was living.

On nights of the harvest moon, the gypsy would spend her evenings on the cliffs of mountains singing in a chorus with the wolves. He voice seemed to melt into their song, if not lead it. It was so beautiful, she was so beautiful, and all Jack could do was sit back and listen in awe. In time Jack began to howl with his lady. They would sit together, naked and pressed against the sun warmed cliffs and howl, voices and spirits entwining as one.

Belly round with child, the gypsy's pace of life did not slow. It was incredible. Though she no longer rode her horses, she mingled with the dogs and made a connection with each. Through all that time her connection with Jack grew stronger and stronger until her need for him was as crucial as his want for her. She knew she could not leave him, but she was unable to leave the spirit world behind. Each passion was so great, it ripped her apart. At times it seemed death would be her only option. It was once said that violent pains accompany violent desires.

They day of birth came on as if it were any other day. Gypsy woman sent Jack out to fetch a root from the woods to aid her labor pains. She did not want him to see the pain that ripped in her body, pain from such a gentle love. When Jack returned to her the sun was setting in the distance, it had taken him most of the day to find that which she called for. He came to her only to find her cold and curled up like a dog, child quietly sleeping in her arms. When she spoke to Jack, her voice trembled with pain and weakness.

She asked Jack to raise their son to be wild and free as she once was. Jack said nothing, just held his breath to hear the dying voice of his love. Inside he knew already that he could not do this. It would be too painful to see her looking back at him through the eyes of a baby. She murmured something of the spirit world and how she was needed there. It was more than the death talk he had heard from brave men and women in their deaths before. She said their child belonged there with her but that he would be forced to walk in both worlds now. She gasped to tell him one final thing when her flame was blown out.

The temperature in the room seemed to drop with the closing of her eyes. Jack stroked her flawless cheek and felt the flesh turn hard.

Tears streamed down his face and spilled onto on the wood floor. Heavy and wet. *Splat. Splat.* She had given him life and now it felt she had taken it as well. With the child still asleep, Jack watched the tiny awkward body wiggle and turn. It would never know his mother's love. Jack winced as he felt his spirit die with his beautiful angel. He knew he would never be the same. Doing so would be too painful.

Outside, as if to mock him, the wolves picked up a tune. Cursing them under his breath, he picked up the child and wrapped him in a blanket. Little did Jack know they sang of welcoming to the child, and of goodbye to one of their own.

Bill went on to talk about the spirit world, a place he visited often. That was where he got the horses, in trade for the sled pups, for so many years. It was another plane of existence and though he could never stay for too long, Bill gathered much strength and wisdom from the lands.

When he disappeared, he went to the spirit lands in search of his mother and all that awaited him... There, all the animals he crossed were champion figures of their earth world counterparts. They were stronger, healthier, and bigger. A team of dogs, who had once been his pups, pulled a sled behind him. He had packed for days and needed help to carry the weight.

Bill met the White Tiger, strongest spirit in all the lands. He later found a wild oak tree that harbored his mother's spirit. She harbored fruit that was intoxicating, like a drug. He would take from her and she would speak to him. She told her son to bring her horses back to his world. They had all run back to the spirit world when her flesh died. They were no longer needed to grace the spirit grounds with their hooves or their presence, at least not all of them. The royal animals that dwelled in the spirit lands once existed on the earth world and once more, a balance needed to be restored. Bill promised to raise his mother's horses and set them free to live on the earth lands once more.

Bill brought his mother's herd of horses to his earth world with no struggle. They loved the man as they had loved the gypsy who was a mother to beasts and in turn, they loved her son. After awhile Bill learned that these horses were special. They were larger, stronger, and always warm to the touch. They ran through drifts of snow with strength and joy as if it were powder from the stars themselves.

The horses were reliable yet they remained untamed. They could not be managed like draft animals, they had to be treated as equals, partners. Rare as unicorns they too were once native to both lands. Old books and pieces of history told of the entire champion animal's presence. Though now man only noted them as myths or legends. Bill was doing his part to introducing them back to his world where they could roam as they once did.

The horses spoke with Bill, as the wolves did to Cara. She was enchanted when Bill told her this. One, because he spoke with animals as she had always dreamed he did. Two, he clearly knew of her, her talents and how she spoke with the animals as well. She figured once he mentioned the White Tiger that it had told him of her. She was curious how many other creatures were aware of her as well.

Bill took a drink from his canteen. His dogs were crawling around the fire pit, licking at smells of dinner the night before. Cara's team watched the other dogs from the sides of their eyes. Their interest however, was focused on the meeting between the two people.

As Cara waited for Bill to go on, she scratched Risk behind his ears. Risk licked his chops eagerly, wanting Bill to keep talking. His words affected him in as many ways as they did Cara. In the background, he could hear Queen romping with Rawhide in the forest. The two were so glad to be together again and Risk was warmed by their comfort.

"My friend Rawhide missed your Queen wolf. You know, she was from the spirit world as well. My mother said they led a pack together though I never knew anything of it."

"Well it seems to show now, doesn't it?"

Laughter grew between the two, the underlying oneness of their souls mirroring that of Ol Jack and the gypsy woman.

"So Bill, it was your mother who sent you here then? Looking for Queen?"

Bill smiled in a way that made Cara's heart skip. Eyes locked with hers, he rose from his knees where he was drinking and stood tall, facing her. Never once did he take his eyes from hers.

"I came here, to find you."

Oh, the words sang beautifully to Cara. This was far too surreal. The bursting thoughts inside her mind were barricaded inside. They managed to be contained when she asked Bill,

"Why?"

"Well, it seems you and I have work to do. Together."

The flesh on her cheeks turned pink. She couldn't help but

blush. What was wrong with her? Why couldn't she keep it together around this man? It didn't help that she was lacking in practice at this.

"There is a place, over a range of mountains not too far off. It is where I always left my brother to pass through the spirit world. You see, there are two passages through those mountains. One will take you where you need to be, with me in the Harvest Valley. The other is the portal to the spirit world. It is only accessible when it calls for you. If the time is not right, the path will lose you in an eternity of hills and cold."

Bill paused to let the words steep into Cara, like tea leaves in hot water. Seeing the woman was still eager to hear more, he went on. He hoped he had not been too forward in his advances but she was his soul mate, he already knew it.

"I must go before you, but I cannot mark a trail. Now that I have found you, it is time to begin my life in the Harvest Valley. It is there that I am to breed, raise, and release my mother's horses. I think they are mystical, and the world has lost so much of its wild magic. Don't you think?"

Bill asked this mostly as an excuse to gaze into her eyes. Swirls of color, swirls of earth. Green from the pines, brown from the earth and striking gold from the sun. In her eyes, he saw the very magic of the wild that he spoke of.

"Well I remember a distant world, years back, where I found little magic. But I can see it these days, in little things. Just flecks though. Things that glisten to me, like mica does in a stone."

Cara was satisfied in the poetry that came out in her answer. It was rare that beautiful prose came out so freely, without her even thinking.

"Sometimes I see it in people, too."
Nodding to Bill, she asked him of what next.

"Well, you must meet me in the valley. I see no other future, really."

Whispering Bill took one step closer. He smelled rich, like dirt, leaves and man. Nodding his head down, he lightly kissed her on the crown of her head. Cara's skin tingled when his warm lips touched her skin.

"When do I go? And I have to take Risk."
"Queen has told my mother he must go, actually."
Risk looked up at Cara and showed his glistening teeth in a

wolfy smile. Cara gave him another scratch behind the ears in satisfaction. Perfect! Another journey together.

"But, how will I find my way? Especially if you cannot leave me a trail."

"Wait for Queen's pups to be of pulling age, and they will guide the way. Risk must lead the team, for his spirit is strongest and will be of much help to the others. But remember, you are not going to the spirit lands. Harvest Valley is on the earth world, but it is tied closely with the spirit world. It's perfect for our kind. Only the strong of body and heart may reach it and survive."

"I see. Now what about Queen's pups? When did this happen? I believe she is too old to carry."

Cara had missed the display of affection put on by Rawhide and Queen during their greeting. Risk had not had time to explain to Cara what he knew. Watching her and Whispering Bill, he felt he knew less and less.

"Rawhide, the alpha of the Harvest valley pack, has been her mate for years. Queen is indeed aging deeply now, just as he is. Many of their years were spent together, after she came to our lands with my mother. And now, she is carrying their last litter. I believe that they mated this morning. Her fertility in such age is a gift from my mother."

The bright sun warming her back made Cara want to curl up with Queen, and share her own joy with the she wolf. Bill's mentioning of Queen's age triggered thought in Cara. She could never pin point Queen's age. Thinking about it, within the past year she had noticed the she wolf begin to slow, signs of the tiring of age. She knew Queen was past the age of birthing pups, that was why she found such joy in mothering the pups of others.

"I must be going Cara. I'd like to set out before the sun dies today. Oh and Queen will be out with Rawhide for half a moon span. Don't worry, they are traveling to my mother so she may bless the seeds and let them grow. See my dogs; I have borrowed them from a medicine man. He is watching over my horses. Now it's time I get them back and take them to our new home.

" *Our* new home?"

"Well of course. You'll be there, and so will I. And isn't it obvious? We are of the same kind."

"We are?"

"We will talk about us later, woman. I just need your word

before I travel. Do I have it?"

"Yes, I will be there."

"Good."

"I am glad to have met you. Oh and good job finding me!"

Cara laughed, for it was *she* who had found *him*, after all.

"Oh I just longed to bring you closer to me, that's all Ms. Sedalia."

"Uh huh."

"I have known about you from the day you began work with my father. Queen messaged the wolves, they told Rawhide, and my mother showed you to me."

"She did?"

"She and the Tiger communicate often. I think she may even be a mother to him, as well."

"I'll see you soon Bill."

"Come back to me in one piece!"

"Of course."

That was all that needed to be said to make Cara grin wildly with excitement. She loved this man, though he didn't even know it yet. Bill began packing up, and Cara turned her back to do the same. When they were both packed and had the dogs hitched up, they exchanged a farewell embrace. His skin was warm to her, hers was soft to him. And with that, the two started off in different directions.

Four
~~~~~~~~~~~~~~~~~~~~~~~~~~~~~~~~

Warm and full, Cara sat with a blanket draped over her shoulders. She was back at her home with Ol' Jack. They sat opposite each other around the fire pit in the center of the room. They had eaten a warm dinner of fresh caribou meat and hot bread she made for the two of them. If Jack still loved anything anymore, he loved Cara's cooking. They were both quiet over dinner, mostly because hunger was the first priority and conversation could wait.

Ol' Jack was tired; he had been working hard on a new totem carving in front of their home. It was to thank the great spirits, but was also a marker of Jack's memories. Without saying anything, Cara studied the tall carving. She realized that there was a figure for each face that Jack had loved. On the bottom, there was a raven for Chuck. Raven because of his untimely death and disappearance. A woman for his wife, a bear for Bill and his masculine build. A wolf for her, and at the very top, a white horse for his truest love, the gypsy lady.

It was growing late into the evening, and Cara just sat quietly. Thinking of the totem pole, she studied Jack's body language and smells. She could feel his pain dripping through his pores. Something had happened while she was gone. Though when asked, Harrington said nothing. Cara began pondering her encounter with Whispering Bill and what she should tell Jack. That is, if she should say anything at all.

Earlier, when the sun was just setting, Cara heard the wolves cry. Looking at Jack, he turned away from her, and she swore he was crying with them. The tear that ran down his nose was wet with the loneliness the wolves' song gave him. After an unusual amount of praise for her cooking, Cara realized the man loved her, and how much her returns really meant to him. Every time she shipped out with the dogs, there was a chance she could never come back.

The changing in the seasons made Cara restless and she found herself called out to dance with the moon and stars. With Risk by her side she would spend evenings out, wild and free, in the forest. Jack Harrington did not approve of Cara's evening runs. He always told her it gave the people a bad impression. In response Cara would wrinkle her nose to the man, like a dog on a bad scent. She didn't like how Jack was reshaping the village.

While she was gone, a group of white men, terrorists in their own way, passed through the village. What they brought with them, their "culture", had found purchase in the weakened mind of Jack Harrington. His loneliness was turning into gullibility, pleased that others from another place were interacting with him. The white men influenced Jack just as they had planned. Though they left before the wild girl Jack spoke of could chase them out of town, with her rumored wolf nipping at their heels. The people in the village liked Cara, the way she was a tangle of human and beast. A balance between a primitive savage and refined young woman, she was also their protector it seemed.

In town the people felt pressured they now had to put forth an image, to maintain a reputation. The white men swore they'd return to monitor the village's "progress". That was of course, if they managed to stay alive as trespassers in NOTR. Someone would find them and destroy them or if given the chance, Cara would. Their poison words sickened her. The things they told her neighbors, that their lifestyles were dirty and uncivilized. Uncivilized to who? These devil men, as she thought it, were lucky not to have lingered here to hover over her people. No, Jack's people.

With things progressing under Jack's unsure guidance, the village would find controversy easily, and drift apart. They were such a strong tribe; it would be a shame to lose that. Harrington was trying to force limits and behavioral guidelines for the people. That was *not* what their nation was about. It pained Cara to see Jack going on like this, deranged in his old age. The village folk followed him and trusted him as their alpha, though skeptical of his judgments.

Putting children to bed at a certain time, reshaping their schedules to the sun rather than to their spirit seemed wrong. These were the types of rules and regulations Cara found pointless. Instinct, she imagined it to be, made her resist the rules and regulations of social domestication. All that was important was health, hunger, and happiness. With her needs restricted, and her head in a crisis, Cara wanted to run. That was all there was to it. No real direction or plans to go anywhere... Just the overwhelming urge to be on the move once more.

When she was out dancing under the moon, she was free of Harrington's rules and the people's dissatisfaction. She liked the way she was and wouldn't change for the world. Not even Bill. It was nights like tonight when the weather was fair and sanctuary could be found that kept her from returning to the village. Things would work themselves out, they had to.

****

Off in the spirit world, Queen ran beside Rawhide, chasing dreams and following their trail of final destiny. The pups she carried kicked and turned inside her as she ran at a slower pace that often made Rawhide snort in frustration. He'd quickly lick her lips in apology, and they would continue their gait. Down hills, through meadows, hunting as they traveled on. The game was plentiful, but fierce. The hunts were always fine, always challenging, and often rewarding.

After crossing back to the earth lands, Rawhide spent many days watching his mate dig relentlessly into the side of a shallow plateau. The overhang shaded the entrance of her den, keeping it cool in the increasing heat of the day. After finishing her project, Queen bathed in the shade in front of her cave, tongue lolling as she waited for Rawhide to return from a hunt.

Dashing through the forest with a marmot in his jaws, Rawhide came to Queen. He went to nuzzle her in greeting but instead, she snarled and Rawhide was forced to drop the food in front of her and step back. He found a boulder just a few feet away from the cavern where he could keep on eye on her while watching the rolling hills freckled with forest. This routine had become familiar to him, for he had been a stud and an alpha for quite some time. Watching Queen disappear into the den, Rawhide closed his eyes and remembered their last litter.

There was a time, before he went to the spirit world with Queen, when they lived in a place decorated by aspen trees, evergreens, blue spruce and pines. Through the valleys, purple columbines and sweet smelling sage waved in the wind. They had a happy pack of five but deaths came through drought and famine. It was then that man and his machines began eating up the land and its inhabitants. Game was scarce and the land could no longer support the pack. Seasons thinned out the weak and only the strong and healthy survived.

With only his mate remaining, Rawhide had to lead them to safety. Some place they could hunt and flourish once more. They never found their paradise. Everywhere they roamed, game was increasingly scarce and certain strokes of the moon brought forth men with guns to take meals from him and his fellow predators. The two wolves roamed across the Rockies and managed to stake out a territory in a place where man-sightings were scarce.

Queen gave a late birth to four healthy, blue-eyed, mewing pups. Rawhide struggled to feed them all, but his muscles became rigid, as well as his determination. He kept his family fed and became an exceptional hunter in the process. Almost to a point where it was easy.

An early winter called out for survival of the fittest. Three pups were lost in less than a week. There was one male pup, downy fur mottled in tones of white and gray who was strong. He alone had survived. A winter snow blew in unexpectedly; all the while the three wolves were hungry. Still too young to hunt, their pup was left in a makeshift den while the adults went out in desperate searches for food.

Shivering and alone, the pup was curled tightly in a ball under a smooth granite boulder. He heard noises. He heard footsteps of some animal, too light for a bear but the creature walked in a pattern that no wolf would carry. The noisy creature climbed on top of the rock he was shaking under. The pup was diseased and afraid. When Rawhide returned to the den, he found his litter was gone, never to be seen again, he thought.

****

The rising of a half moon reminded Cara of the village, swallowed in a half of darkness. The tranquility of her solitude brought her many profound thoughts while distracting her from her responsibilities and duties. She hadn't been down to the village in days and she couldn't help but feel that things down there were getting worse.

A few days past, a young blond child stumbled upon them out in the woods. Cara was dozing off with her head on Risk's haunch when the girl clumsily threw a rock that nearly struck Risk in the head. Risk knew she was only trying to get their attention so he didn't dash off. He had heard the girl coming but thought her no threat. Her light, steady trudge through the forest was barely heavier that than of a young fawn. The girl scurried down the hill and charged into Cara's arms. Cara held the child and felt cold tears dampen the skin where her blouse should be.

The girl cried, and explained her search to Cara.

"No one else knew where to find you! But I knew. And I'm so glad I found you."

The little girl was heaving in sobs. They seemed to be a mixture of fear, sadness, helplessness and excitement. Cara furrowed her brow and released her embrace.

"Hush, little one. Clam down and quiet yourself. Its okay, hush....Now, who is looking for me?"

The little girl breathed in, choking on her air a few times. Cara lifted the chin of the child and gazed into her brown eyes. They were so dark, barely distinguished from the pupil. After gazing into the wolf woman's eyes, the child regained her composure and spoke in little more than a whisper.

"Cara, the wolves have come and I think they are searching for you. No one knows what to do so everyone went out looking for you. It's so strange."

"What is?"

"See, Chief Harrington just sits on his porch and watches the wolves. He doesn't do anything, or talk to any of us. He is very angry."

"Well why do you think he is angry? Especially if the wolves aren't doing anything. That's good for us, right honey?"

"Yeah, I know. The wolves aren't killing and they leave us people alone."

"And the dogs?"

"They leave them alone too. The only thing they do in town is walk around your cabin in circles. It's weird. What is happening?"

About that time, the little blond girl began to work herself up again. Starting with sniffles that turned into tears, the child began to wail.

"Oh please, come back Cara! Please, please, please, please! Everyone is grumpy and my mom and daddy don't like Mr. Harrington anymore. No one does! They all say he has gotten a dark heart. And now no one knows what to do! I don't know what to do! I don't know where to go, but I don't like the way things are there!! Come help! Pleeaasee."

Cara just listened as she wiggled and whined and pleaded to her more. It was clear she was no older than ten. Cara hugged the child once more and cooed her back to calm.

"Alright, alright. It's ok, nitanish."

Cara used the native word for daughter when comforting the child. That alone brought a smile to her little brown eyes. All she needed was comfort and support. The feeling that someone was there for her. Cara remembered the feeling.

She had told the child she would go back by the half moon and bring back the light to Jack's heart. She hated to admit it, but Cara loved playing the hero. Also, she was very good at it. After talking for a while and playing a bit of tag, Cara let the girl pat Risk before sending her back home. The children of the community seemed to get a thrill from the big wolf at Cara's side. Touching him seemed to be quite the privilege.

When the half moon arrived, Cara realized she didn't want to go back. She was happy out here. They were free to live as they wanted and do as they pleased. The mild season made the days warm and the nights especially pleasant. She had food, she had water and she had Risk. That was all she felt she needed.

As the moon crawled farther up into the sky, Cara sang with Risk. Their howls echoed the hills and drifted to the village. A great horned owl chimed into her song, hooting in the breaks of their voice. Partly, Cara sang to the people below because tonight, she planned return. Queen and Rawhide would be there, waiting for them. That put butterflies in Cara's stomach. If the timing was right, there would be puppies awaiting their arrival. She couldn't wait!

A gentle rain began to fall, and Cara and Risk took off. Running tonight was grand. It was both late at night and early in the morning, and the soil smelled rich from the rain. Wide eyed and grinning, Cara and Risk were side by side, bodies breathing and stretching. Two figures in constant graceful motion. She loved their silhouettes.

For a human, Cara had exceptional night vision. For a wolf, she was little more than blind. But the cool of the night was something she loved, and had learned to adapt to. Other senses kicked in and she was keen on her scents and sounds. It was another world in the dark. Different creatures stirred in different ways in the voodoo spells of the night.

****
****

A rising sun was enough to celebrate back in the village. It was just recently that the sun had returned from its five month absence. The light filled up the human soul, making it dance and sing in joy. Boys and girls of the village rattled instruments and pounded on drums. Women and men sang and danced in a greeting of the sun. They were welcoming it back and giving thanks for they day-star's return. The sun brings life and something equally important to mankind. Bluntly stated, the sun brings joy.

Just outside the village, Cara could hear the music. Her feet hit the earth with the rhythm of the drums. Men and woman cheered when they saw her in the distance. They welcomed her as they did the sun, with chants, whoops, words and dance. She came to them like a vision; the outline of a feral woman, beauty and power with each stride. Beside her galloped a wolf with eyes that glowed like the sun.

They were coming towards the people, running a straight trail to the village road with the bright yellow ball of life at their backs. Truly they were a morning vision that was only recognized through the legends and tales that were told on mystical, starlit evenings. Times when words filled with belief would mingle and entwine with the flames of fire. Until, at last, the spoken images were conveyed in the winding, spiraling, wisps of smoke from the fire.

Greeted with cheers and embraces, Cara joined in the dancing, festivities, and in the food. Risk watched, lingering only for the promise of a meal. Stretched out beside a bench log, Risk took in the surroundings of the village. This was no longer his home but he felt to be, somehow, a piece of his territory. The smell of man had seemed to permanently imbed itself in the grounds of the village. Licking his lips anxiously, he took off to find Cara.

The whirling of people along with their hoots and cries made Risk nervous as he dashed through the swarms of people. He spotted Cara, walking his way with food in her hands. She held a large bone with meat that dripped with hot fat from the grill. She placed the leg on the ground and put her hand on his fuzzy head. She got that just for him and wanted him to realize it. Risk wagged his tail and licked her arm until she giggled enough to drop the flank. With utter contentment, Risk took his gift and walked behind a small hut to eat in privacy. Cara returned to the people after seeing no sign of Jack Harrington in the crowd.

After eating, Risk peered from behind the shack to see where Cara had gone. She was still talking and enjoying the company of the town folk. Preferring not to bother her, Risk turned his back to her and headed towards the cabin. He heard Harrington stirring about inside and decided not to disturb the old man.

Outside, the dogs were quiet, which was not typical of them. Especially with the people making the amount of noise that they were. Padding across the front porch, Risk went to the side of the cabin. Still, it was quiet. Then, with ears up and paws spread wide to silence his stride, the wolf stalked back towards the yard where his team mates still lived.

Risk saw a pile of multi-colored fur to his left. Nine dogs sleeping. They must have had a heavy run last night. To his right, Risk panned up and down the fence for trouble. From his side, all seemed to be quiet and still. Or, did something just dart between the trees? It looked like something dark and fuzzy. Risk watched the fence a moment longer until something heavy knocked his left haunch out from beneath him. It felt like being hit by a train.

It was Bomber, a fully grown malamute-mastiff mix who had never grown out of his puppy stage. The dog knew nothing but pulling and play. This was rather amusing considering the fact that Bomber was, with no contest, the largest member of the team. Of any team Risk had seen, for that matter. Bomber even towered taller than most wolves, and was thick as a bear. He was a mean-looking beast but harbored the least bit of cruel intent, other than bullying others at playtime. Risk just so happened to walk in as the perfect target for his game.

Swirling into a pivot, Risk spun around to meet Bomber eye to eye for a stare down. Within seconds Bomber lost interest, pulling his body weight back for a full weighted catapult launch on Risk. Brains always beat brawn in face-offs like this. Risk faked right and maneuvered left leaving Bomber with a bloody chin and a snout full of gravel. Risk was closing in on his target when Heron, the alpha dog, stuck his head out of the large barn-like shelter.

Risk felt the intensity of his stare and stopped short to look and listen. Behind him, Risk heard Bomber whine. Playtime had been canceled. After pawing the ground, Bomber lumbered off. Disappointed he was left with nothing else to do. Heron barked a short yip, beckoning Risk to come inside. Something was wrong.

Five
~~~~~~~~~~~~~~~~~~

The shelter was a 5 x 16 mini-barn made from thick, heavy wood and was filled with sweet smelling hay. The opening to get inside was skinny, allowing only one dog to enter at a time. Heron was in the doorway, blocking others from leaving or entering the shed. Risk greeted Heron with a worried whine, deep in his throat. For admission purposes, he bowed his head, but did not cower in submission. Heron raised his hair and doubled his size, purely from instinct, upon their greeting. He sniffed Risk deeply, puffing his breath down to the warm pinks of his flesh. Then Heron turned back into the barn with Risk following at his heels.

Queen was in the back corner. Her eyes were half closed and she was panting with exhaustion and fear. Three bitches hovered around her. She wheezed while licking a dead pup, still at her tit. The air was heavy with the salty, metallic stench of blood. There was the rich, dark blood form her pups as well as thin blood from somewhere else. There was a wound deep in her shoulder. The walls seemed to melt around Risk as he made sense of it all. Queen, was dying.

A spark of faith gleamed in Queen's dark auburn eyes when she saw Risk across the room. He went to her, despite a glare from Heron and snorts from the females. They moved aside as Risk cowered in front of Queen, his wolf mother, whining in fear of loosing her. Nosing her muzzle, Risk tried to raise her head. Queen snarled and snapped at him, stopping all potential efforts he might have made to try and save her. Still whining like a pup, Risk flattened his ears to his head and let out a long alto note. A sob.

"This is how it is to be Risk. My death is timely. My two pups are alive, you are here and Cara will raise my pups as she has you. The only thing wrong is...." Queen struggled for breath, inhaling in short, and sharp breaths. Rib cage wide with air, she then hacked the air up, along with a skinny stream of bile from her empty stomach. Risk only crooned softly as he waited. What was it that had gone wrong? He wanted her to tell him, so he could find Cara, and tell her. Together, they'd fix everything. He just needed Queen to tell him.

"The man...he shot me."

"The man?"

Queen had always had a soft spot for the human Jack; she always called him by his name. Never "the man". That was what unhappy or rebellious dogs called him. But never Queen. She always ran well for Jack and in return, Jack always took especially good care of her. All this made no sense to the young wolf. Why would Jack shoot Queen? Something *had* to be wrong. Instead of speaking out, fast and filled with questions like Cara would have, Risk just listened. Perhaps because he had nothing to say or, because he was too wise to speak at all.

"He shot at Rawhide too. I don't know if he got him. Once Rawhide backed off, he shot me. And, he took two of my pups. I came in here to safely deliver my third...."

Her voice trailed off. None had mentioned that her third happened to lack a heartbeat. Although she licked the cooling pup as if it did. To Risk, it still didn't register why a care giver would take from the life he had provided. A wave of impact crashed in Risk's brain. He cocked his head as the truth surged through him.

Jack shot Queen. Jack shot Rawhide. Claws digging into the wood, his heart beat loud with panic and anger. Risk wasn't sure why, but he was just as upset about Rawhide as he was Queen. His muscles flinched. Time to move, his instinct told him. Bending down on his belly once more, Risk licked Queen's nose and promised her his return. He had to get Cara. Queen's eyes shut in a smile, never to open again.

The gray wolf exploded out of the shelter. His mouth flung open only to reveal his massive canines shining white against the background of mauve, the inside of his mouth. The rest of the dogs were pacing amongst each other inside the pen. The sleeping dogs lay unphased, exhausted in their pile of fluff.

Risk's paws beat the ground like the rhythm of the people's drums. The path through town was uncrowded, giving Risk all the space he needed to pick up speed as he ran. Reaching the end of the village where the festivities had been, Risk was relieved when he saw how much the crowd had thinned. The people were in their sweat lodges and sewing circles, enlightening their spirits in one way or another.

Cara was sitting on a log bench, telling stories to a large group of little children. This did not stop Risk or even slow him down. Most children of the village liked the dogs here; a wolf to them was no different. Wheeling to a stop in front of Cara, Risk turned his face to greet the children with a puppy-like smile. The children laughed and cheered, though none got up to touch him. He was thankful for that.

Turning back to face Cara, he pored out his information on the recent events. Her eyes got wide as he spoke to her, then narrowed tightly as he finished. Cara politely excused herself from the children, promising to finish the tale before long. After a farewell hug from each child, Cara spun on her heels and burst down the wide strip of path through the village.

Running with the dogs and wolves had kept Cara's speed up. Her pace was quick, her steps were light. With each stride she covered more ground than the fastest runners of the village. Risk shot in front of her, heading to the cabin. He planned to search for the movement he thought he had seen outside the fence, just moments ago.

Before going indoors, Cara ran to the shed. She poked her head inside and was greeted by bared teeth and wild snaps from a young female. The dog got nothing but air, though her teeth were just inches away from Cara's face. Pulling out, and then ducking inside once more, Cara crammed her body inside the shed. She knocked the dog on her side from the sheer momentum of her weight forced through the doorway. Looking at the dog, Cara grabbed her scruff and pulled her to the door commanding,

"OUT! NOW!"

After sending the dog scampering out with her tail tucked tightly between her legs, Cara looked to the end of the shed. Her attention turned to Queen and the lifeless form of the newborn pup. Neither of them moved, not even so much as a twitch. It was still and quiet. Queen was dead and Cara was alone.

Wasting no time, Cara pulled with all her might to get Queen out of the shelter. The wolf was heavy in her former life and as Cara lifted her, her weight seemed to double. Sliding her arms under the body, Cara scooped Queen up into her arms. Muscles ripping, veins pulsing, her legs screamed with every lunge towards the cabin. Though her body resisted the abuse, her mind powered over, backed up by adrenaline and Cara kept on.

She staggered to the front of the cabin, breathing heavily. She inhaled, the warm scent of Queen's blood and fur filling her lungs. The woman swallowed another gulp of power, given to her by the death of her friend. Turning the knob with her left hand, Cara kicked the door open the rest of the way and barged in.

"Jack?!"

Her voice was hoarse with anger and choked up sobs. She would not let the sorrow from her loss pour out just yet. When testing times came, she often built a dam inside her self. It held back all the feelings and emotions until they got so strong that the dam would break, sending tears gushing out like waterfalls. Sometimes, like today, the dam would spring little leaks when the pressure was too great for even the thickest wall to hold back.

"Jack?"

Cara called softer this time. She hadn't even walked into the house yet. She just stood in the doorway, holding the wolf carcass. Blood began dripping into the wood of the house, splattering with each red drop. Cara quieted herself and tried to listen. It was as if her breath and the pounding of her heart was all she could hear.

Arms quaking now from the strain of Queen's weight, Cara closed her eyes and listened once more. Outside her body there was whimpering. Little whelps whimpering and whining upstairs in Jack's room. Of course. It was the only room Cara never cared to venture into. Well, she thought, there should be a first time for everything.

Angry that Jack wouldn't answer her, Cara dropped Queen's dead body on the floor. It hit with a heavy *thud*. Arranging her face in a scowl no man could forget, Cara's rage shifted from the major crisis to the minor inconvenience. She really didn't want to go upstairs but, she had to go to Jack's room to solve the problem.

Sneaking up the stairs, as if he wouldn't have heard her on arrival, she made her way to his room. The door was open a crack, enough to see inside. Poking her head into his room she saw Jack's old, weary profile. He was sitting on the edge of his bed, which was lined with a wooden frame much like the one in her room. The walls were bare save for two pictures of two different women. Cara couldn't recognize the other, but one was her for sure. When had he gotten a picture of her?

The room smelled of old skin and illness. Ol' Jack had aged much since she last saw him. The lines cut beneath his gray eyes indicated days of pain and grief. Though his brows were scowling, he was smiling calmly. Looking down to Harrington's lap, Cara saw the two squealing pups that had been making all the noise. One was feeding from a bottle while the other wriggled across Jack's lap, burying itself in a bloodied towel. These were Queen's pups and Jack was caring for them as he had once taught Cara to do.

Revising her tactics of approach, Cara calmed herself. Breathing deeply she squished the leaky emotions back behind her dam and patched it with a fake smile. Because Jack had become clearly unstable, the last thing she wanted to do was upset him further. His actions had grown far too unpredictable.

Stepping lightly, Cara drifted across the floor until she was side by side with Jack. The old man turned his haggard face to her, a tear dangling on the duct of his right eye.

"Ain' they somethin? All little and curled up like this?"

Jack's voice was crinkly, as voices of the elders often are.

"Sure is Jack."

Watching the pups, a real smile penetrated Cara's fake cover grin. She turned to find a clean towel on the bedside table. Picking the towel up in one hand and a pup in the other, she brought them together. The wolf cubs needed a mother and needed her milk. With Queen dead it would be tricky to find another lactating female canine.

The other pup had stopped feeding and now looked blindly at the Jack's human face staring down at him.

"I need the other one Jack. And, we need to find them a mother, because Queen's dead."

Rage pricked the second half of her sentence. As if Jack didn't know. He was the one who shot at Queen and Rawhide in the first place. At least that's how Risk relayed it. Animals didn't lie, not like man does. Deception is one thing. Lies are another.

"I know these aren't dog pups Cara."

"Yeah? I bet."

All the tenderness Cara had seen in Jack was gone, snapped shut by the jaws of ugly hurt and cruel words. None the less, he handed the pup to Cara, and she proceeded to clean and inspect it as she had the first. Swallowing the venom from his words, Jack went on,

"Some son-of-a-bitch wolf was rummaging around our cabin. I turned my back missy, I left him alone. 'Till I seen him prowling inside the fence and nipping at Queen. So I go in, get my gun, and shoot 'em. Nicked good too, enough to bleed him dry I 'magine."

Cara burst in to interrupt, her voice loud to the ears of the deaf pups.

"So you shot Queen and took her pups? Jack she's dead now! If nothin' else you knew she was our best dog!"

"She ain' no dog missy, I seen it in her eyes more than ever. That bitch was a wolf. She gone crazy while you were gone. I only shot her to slow her down, she was bitin' at everything! Even the thin air, she was rabid!"

"I doubt it Jack. Now you've killed her and taken her pups. You realize you've left them with no mother?! This is out of hand, Jack. And I know about the gypsy woman and about the wolves and I know-"

Jack Harrington tore out of the room. Stairs heaved under his stomping feet and the door flung open once more. Cara wrapped the pups quickly in a small nest of towels Jack had put out on the floor. She threw herself off the bed to follow after Jack.

She stopped short at the totem pole in front of the cabin. Glancing at it, she noticed that it had been beautifully carved and painted. It was complete. Perhaps now Ol' Jack was too.

Back to the chase, there was no sign of Harrington anywhere. Looking back and forth there was no powder to capture tracks. There came a howl from Risk, followed by another male's voice. It sounded wounded, it had to be Rawhide. Cara ran to them, beckoned by their call. They met in the middle of town, the large shaggy wolf known as Rawhide hid a limp as he arrived behind Risk.

"Where did he shoot you?"

"Cara I'm fine. It really doesn't matter now anyway. I've lost Queen, I can feel it."

"But two of your pups are alive, Rawhide. Now come with me, I was going after Jack but he can wait. I'm taking care of you."

"No."

"At least for the night. Listen I need your help now that Queen is gone."

Cara turned to walk towards the cabin. As Risk began to stroll by her side, Rawhide sat down. He refused to go with them. Swirling back around, Cara went back to Rawhide. He continued to speak.

"I know she's gone but it was her time. Soon it will be mine."

"But-"

"I will help you. I am going to find Jack. I need to meet with him. He knew me and I know him."

"Then why did he shoot at you?"

This time it was Risk who jumped in the conversation. He asked the very question that was on the tip of Cara's own tongue.

"Because it was love who killed his mate and my bond with Queen was something he envied. So he took away my love. Now, death is due for the both of us. Take care of my family Cara."

With that Rawhide lifted his muzzle to the clouds. He sniffed the wind to find Jack's trail. He would have to go into the village.

"Don't' worry, all will be done before the rising of the next morning sun."

Risk looked to Cara. She was looking at him. Together they headed back to the cabin.

"That was my father you know."

Risk wagged his tail as he spoke, yellow eyes gazing dreamily up to Cara. She didn't speak, she didn't have to. Instead, when night came, they howled. Out in the woods there was blood on the dirt and peace in the air. Jack Harrington slowly passed away. In his hand, he grasped the paw of a dying wolf.

Six

~~~~~~~~~~~~~~~~~~~~~~~~~~~~~~

Granite and Aqua loved their lives at the cabin. They loved the dogs, their brother Risk and Cara, even more. The brothers were always together, even as they blossomed from puppy hood. Granite was brown eyed, bearing black and white markings similar to those of a husky's. Litter mate Aqua was the common color of a gray wolf. Muted tones of white, gray, and tan created the perfect camouflage in this region. Aqua got his name from his eyes; they kept the same shade of blue that was given to him at birth, though he did not lack the ability to see.

Both pups were fair tempered, while far from docile. Granite's size and strength over-powered Aqua's, while the smaller brother compensated with speed and remarkable navigational skills. He could track any trail. Proof was when they tagged along in the forest with Risk and Cara. As wolflings often do, they would occasionally stray and get lost. While Granite would search and howl for Risk, Aqua would take the lead and find Cara with relative ease. Any obstacles in the way had to deal with the mass and power of Granite. The two ran through the forest, as close to unstoppable as two wolves could be. Together they were a powerful combination.

In the village, a new town leader had not been decided upon. With the loss of Jack Harrington, the people were unsure of what to do. Many members of the village nominated Cara, knowing her knowledge and guidance would serve them well. People viewed her as a protector, a bridge to the world of the wolf and bear. When she was around no harm came to them from the wild.

Though she was flattered, Cara had to refuse their offer. She could not stay here the rest of her life. She had so much more to see and do. The people would have to lead one another. When seeking knowledge, healing and advice, the medicine men and women would be the ones to call on until a new leader was decided upon.

The cabin was now hers though it no longer seemed to suit her. She felt too closed in, preferring to live outdoors in the kinder seasons. But Cara stayed to raise Queen's pups to pulling age as was requested. While she focused on Granite and Aqua, she maintained her place in the village. She made delivery runs and began training a young man who was quite taken with the dogs, the sport and most importantly, the wolves. The village needed someone like him to replace her when she left them behind.

Her new student took over Jack's room and filled the house with a new, warm scent. He watched over the dogs when Cara took the wolves out to run. He tended to the team as she imagined Bill would have once done. Quiet, humble and content in his work. He was great. The dogs ran well for him, and she would often peek out her window to find him playing with the dogs as if he were one of them. It made her wonder if he shared her abilities to live as one of *them.*

An easy year slid by, bringing age to the wolflings and Cara all the same. The brothers were now old enough to leave. Every evening when Cara was out with Risk, Aqua and Granite, she felt an overwhelming sense of family. Something so warm, and so safe, she was sure she had never felt anything like it before.

This was her pack. She was their family. With the rising of the sun season, Cara and her wolves left the village behind, it was time to move on. In time she would miss the village, she had learned so much. She packed a sled with only that which she would need on the journey to Harvest Valley. Risk in lead, the wolves pulled the sled with amazing power, strength and speed. The last the people of Harrington's village heard of Cara and her wolves was the howling of four voices, singing goodbye.

****

The Journey

In the quiet of the first night on the trail, Cara shut her eyes and thought of Whispering Bill. Questions of the future flooded her brain. Would he be there? When? What if he wasn't there? What if she couldn't get there? How long would it take to be there? What if she entered the Spirit world? Would she and the pack get lost in a vortex of utter nothingness? What would that be like? Was that death? Would others be there? Perhaps there would be creatures whose bodies had been swirled together and walked in a skin of discolored fur and flesh. Spiraling into her imagination, Cara began to dream.

Beasts with eyes as pale and blank as the full moon stared at her while her arms were torn from their sockets. Her teeth fell out, hair growing in her mouth where enamel had been. She watched as her pack slipped away, howling until their mouths were equally disfigured. The pack's howls became snorts, oinks, grunts and whines. Gasping, she watched their eyeballs fall from their sockets and stare at her as they rolled away into the emptiness.

Cara tried to scream, but couldn't breathe. Emptiness dragged her lungs into her belly, deflated balloons deprived of air. There grew an emptiness that pulled at her. She was nothing, had no one, and was no where. Cara saw herself translucent, swirling like a rapid deep beneath a river. Then in a blink it was gone, and her eyes opened.

She had dosed off in the seat of the sled. Wide awake, Cara looked around to get her bearings. The wolves pace had slowed down to a trot, still following the invisible trail, the path Bill used to take once upon a time ago. Wheels were on the jig; Cara had the skis nailed along side in case of snowy weather. For now the beasts were gone.

Beneath her the ground turned and groaned. Blinking as if she had something in her eye, Cara tried to clear the visions from her head. Surely they were no more than her psyche scolding her for pressing it too hard, sometimes that happened. Her brain did not digest her thoughts fully and left them to her subconscious to dispose of. If it was too much, fear would come to scour her mind clear. Fear was like bleach. Maybe that's why so many churches were white, she thought.

It was true; she had been neglecting herself over the past month. Her focus was on her escape route rather than her vessel. Finally the mental and emotional discharge she had pushed away was finally catching up with her. All the deaths of those she loved, that had to be it. Or, perhaps it was just time to stop. Cara preferred the later option. Maybe if the pack was not too tired they could all go roam the forest for a while. Maybe even hunt. It had been a long while since they last ran free.

Nothing brings a wolf pack together like a hunt. Running through the forest, branches slashing at her hot skin, Cara had not a care in the world. All she could focus on was the hunt. This was where she belonged, the life she was meant to live. Years of human indifference had only encouraged her to turn to the wild ways of the "savages".

Flashes of fur raced passed her into a clearing. The wolf boys were on to something. Cara's heart continued to pound. Exhaustion meant nothing now that the fire of thrill had arrived. Cara howled to the pack, and to the lone moose she saw across the field.

She sang the wolves a plan to surround the old cow. The prey had not yet seen her canine killers so Cara thought she ought to warn her. That and she loved watching the panic of prey. It reminded her of the fear of death so many creatures have. She would never accept it; to her death was nothing to fear.

Feeling her limbs pull to the earth, Cara's body yearned to become that of a wolf. Her mind was already there and her body wanted to be there with it. Disappointed after feeling nothing, Cara was sure she remained human. She did not appear as such to the old cow down the hill. Seeing Cara, her eyes widened, straining to absorb any and all moonlight. The moose panicked and blindly loped into a patch of thicket.

Nipping at her heels, she was certain the cow was lost in the brush after hearing breaking branches and kicked-up twigs. Cara slowed her panting, heart trying to burst free of its rib-cage prison. Cara revealed a dangerous smile showing all her teeth. She had practically delivered the pack's meal. All had gone to plan as the moose ran through the tangle of thicket. Behind the brush, three hungry wolves waited for their dinner.

Cara made her way through the thicket, following the trampled terrain left by the moose. At last the trail led to its destination, the meal. Risk's head had vanished inside the dead cow's ribcage. To the side, Granite and Aqua whimpered and whined, anxiously awaiting their turn at the dinner table. All packs have hierarchies, even this one. To them Risk was alpha, so he ate first.

Having Cara around threw a wild card into things, instinct clashed with obedience. Often times Risk wondered if he were to act like a wolf or a dog. Wolf always won, but Cara was alpha, even to him. She had raised him, given him his strength and never shown a single sign of weakness. She was a strong alpha so in the eyes of a wolf, she would keep the pack strong as well. She needed to be nourished to nourish the family.

Approaching the still warm carcass, it reeked of blood and flesh. Bloody and pungent with death, it was appetizing none the less. Cara looked down at the gray rump and wagging tail protruding from the beast's belly. Crouching onto her knees Cara let out a low growl, teasing and mocking her wolf.

He had led the others well in the hunt. Though this beast was weak with illness and age, the pack did a good job taking her down, it was fast. Tail still wagging, Risk was not responding to Cara's bullying. He was lost in the pleasure, the victory and the blood. She punched Risk on the thigh, hard enough to get his attention. Risk pulled his head out to stare at her with pupils dilated with ecstasy and bloodlust. His fur was stained red, dripping blood. His lips were pulled pack as far as they could in a wolfy smile of overload.

Cara wanted food. Her belly lurched and turned with anticipated hunger. Still Risk didn't move. He wanted to play. Risk wanted her to tackle him, as she often did, and roll around with him in the dry dirt that drank up the blood. Risk was overwhelmed with joy from their hunt and he did not think of Cara's hunger. Seeing herself reflected in the gleam of Risk's eye, for a moment Cara forgot her hunger too.

She gave in to his tease, tackling him and pushing his nose into the earth. While they wrestled and chased each other, the brothers would sneak back to the carcass and tear off chunks of food for themselves. This didn't last long, however. Cara's hunger ended their romp and the wolf woman proceeded to back to her kill.

Risk paced back and forth by the carcass, all of it for show, trying to get Cara to play again. His distractions made her growl and bare her teeth to him. She yearned to return to the fire and cook her meal. Growling as she had, her stomach agreed. She knew she could not take the whole animal back, but a fat cut of meat would do. Besides, taking a fresh kill to the same place she slept, was just asking for a predator attack. Cara drew her knife from the strap at her side. Her hands were trembling with pleasure and exhaustion. Her muscles screamed for more oxygen and she became light headed.

Falling to her rump, she sat still and breathed. In came the smells that intoxicated the nerves throughout her body. Sweat. Wolf. Meat. Woods. Closing her eyes, Cara stroked the fur of the moose and gave thanks. The fur was thick, heavy and warm. Tomorrow with the light to assist her, she would take some. Now she needed the animal's meat more than her skin to comfort her.

She cut back the skin from the left rear haunch. Blood poured warm down her hands and arms as her claw-of-man sliced through layers of fat and meat. Cara cut herself a thick, heavy steak to take back to camp. It would be enough for dinner and breakfast. Chunk of meat in one hand, knife in the other, Cara turned and made her way back to the sled.

The brothers still had not been able to eat their full and when Cara left the carcass, Risk returned to continue feeding. Watching him eat lazily while their hunger raced through their bones was torture. They would return to the kill when he was done. For now their bodies called for sleep.

Risk was once more engulfed in the moose's body. He pulled his torso out of the ribcage only to see the brothers looking back at him. He had a squishy organ in his mouth and he shook it hard, back in forth like a pup with a chew toy. The brothers knew it would be a while. Risk was having entirely too much fun with his supper.

The morning dawned with an abundant shower of warmth. The breeze was tame; the sun was bright as it stretched across the sky. Still asleep, Cara's fingers were entwined in the black fur of Granite's shaggy scruff. Risk was pouting near by, paws folded and awake with one eye open. Last night when he returned, he went to snuggle up beside Cara. Risk was denied due to his rancid smell which he, of course, didn't think was too bad. So all night he had pouted, hoping she'd change her mind. Unfortunately, it was too nice a day to sleep in and she'd miss his display. With the sun up she would be awake any moment.

Once the pack was up and about, the sun shone victoriously atop a mountain. It was the peak of the morning and all the birds were up to celebrate in a chorus of melodies of chirps and chatters. Cara undid the steak she had tied to a high branch on a tall tree near by. It was untouched and ready for the flame. As she roasted her meal like a cave person would have once done, Risk gnawed on a juicy leg bone he had brought to camp. When Granite and Aqua returned, the bone would be fully stripped of flesh and used as a toy.

Thus became life. The pace was slow, the weather was fair, and the going was easy. On the nights of the full moon the pack would sing joyous songs of the trail and their triumphs. The sun was kind and the moon was magical in all its pale glory. Many cries they sang to her, giving thanks to Lady Luna.

Crossing wolf territory had not yet become a real problem. Around the old village, the wolves used the land as a transitional place. No pack really called that place home. It was shared territory. In the summer, when the game fled to the valley, wolves would call out to warn and frighten another pack if they planned to stay for awhile. Now, things were different. Cara wasn't driving dogs anymore. She was living with wolves, as a wolf, and traveling with her pack. Out here, the pack posed a threat to every predator they came across.

Luckily, the few wolves they had run into throughout the months were only strays and their scents were never too strong. Often they only said,

"I'm here. I'm a Wolf. But I don't really have a home or a family. I don't want to fight."

And so, they were able to move on.

The pack knew where they were going, having no boundaries and no limits. Throughout their journey, the wolves did not keep to themselves as they would have if on business back then. Instead evenings were filled with hunts, songs, and games of tackle and chase. On days when they were not on the move, Cara filled the air with smoke and smells of sweet cooked things. Everywhere the pack was they made themselves at home, regardless of the consequences.

Life was so good out here. There was so much love in her family. Though the weather was warm, the four always slept together, curled up in big tangle of heat. Cara breathed in the smells of this world, *Her* world.

Though she as though she were on vacation, she still dreamed of the Tiger. There was never a time she could forget the sights she had seen of the atrophying earth and its pain. Out here, things were getting better, back in balance. With her back to the earth, she could feel it. The land spoke to her, and she talked back. The earth embraced Cara every time she lay on its plush soil to rest.

Gazing at the stars, Cara felt their healing lights filled the pores of her body with a glistening white magic. She was healthy, she was whole, she was happy. Closing her soft almond eyes, Cara gracefully drifted away into a deep sleep.

Seven
~~~~~~~~~~~~~~~~~~~~~~~
A season had gone by since Cara left the village. In all that time, she had not seen another human. Cara supposed she was okay with that. It hadn't bothered her until she thought about it. It just didn't seem to bother her. Besides, they were getting closer to the valley.

It was the belly of summer, filled with growing plants and trees for the autumn harvest. Berries were ripe and Cara spent hours harvesting the sticky treats, carrying them in a makeshift knapsack made from her leather britches. Cara was fine with the tools used for mending and sewing. Though despite her skills, she still preferred to run around naked. She was a free spirit and did not desire clothing to restrict her flesh.

The itch and clingy-ness of cloth was a persistent memory from her past, even the common attire in the village drove her to bare her body. She didn't like clothes. Clothing looked good on her, but she did not like them, even for ceremony. Cara would paint her face but refused to wear the headdress.

Cara figured the only thing clothes were good for was if they served a function. In the winter, keeping warm but for runs and hunts, restricting the artworks of the flesh so that they would not get in the way. Cara wore a wide strap of leather tied tight across her breasts while she ran with the wolves. Thorns did slash and tear at her skin but she did not care. Her blood dried with the red and blue juices of the fruits she foraged. She was fully exposed to the earth, making herself vulnerable to nature as it was to man.

****

One particular evening Cara found herself struggling to stay awake with the setting of the sun. She stopped the team, to see whether they should continue or rest. It felt as if they were almost there. So close in fact, that the last obstacle remaining was the mountain range that separated the Spirit lands from Harvest valley. If they stopped tonight, they would reach the mountains first thing in the morning. If they kept on, they could be in the middle of the range by the same time.

Cara unhooked the wolves and rubbed them down to check for muscle strains, pains, or injuries. Granite washed Cara's face with a warm, pink tongue. His attempt to wash the sleep off her failed, as Cara was still tired. Aqua imitated human speech to Cara, trying to get a rise out of her. It had worked before. He growled deep in his belly and opened his mouth in round shapes. His words came out in R's and O's. Cara laughed in a huff of breath. The sight and sound of this display was hilarious, but her desire to sleep muted the comedy of Aqua's act.

Bending down to her knees, Cara sat in front of Risk and gazed into his eyes.

"Ok puppy. So what do you want to do?"

Even in his head, Cara's voice was slow and dreamy, like that of a child fresh from a nap.

"Well, were all fed and rested still. We'll keep on for a while longer. We want to get closer."

"Are ya sure?"

"I know you're tired. Relax, go rest in the sled. We will take care of you and ourselves."

"You're the best, wolfy. Thank you."

Months before, Cara would have never dozed off in the sleigh. But being with the safety of her pack, she was able to rest when her mind allowed. Tonight, it would. Her body was full with berries, fish and roots of sweet tasting flowers. The call of autumn was only weeks away and her body wanted to replenish for the oncoming darkness of winter.

Cara stood and asked her brothers,

"Is that all right? I hope Risk isn't pulling my tail. So, I can sleep while you all run?"

Though the pack could speak with Cara just fine, this time they chose to bark and wag their tails in agreement. Some things were just easier.

The wolves went to empty their systems and fill up with a bit of jerky Cara had dried. Then she re-hooked them to their harnesses, and they were off with a lunge. The promise of the valley called to all of them, pulling in their bellies and chests. Curled up under one of Bill's old blankets, she buried her nose into the fabric. At times she could swear that she could still smell Bill's scent. Cara chewed sleepily on a slice of jerky in the sled. The fit was snug, but she could sleep comfortably enough as they bounced and rattled toward the mountains.

Eyes bobbing open and closed, Cara watched as the scenery fled behind her. Trees, hills, bushes and an owl. Then her eyelids closed, leaving a warm, familiar darkness. Her eyes turned inward as she looked at the beauty and the depth of her own soul.

Outside, the ground began to climb upward. The wolves simultaneously smiled as they approached the mountains. The light of the moon tickled in Risk's belly. A new feeling was coming over him; it was a feeling of control, responsibility and leadership. It felt good.

The padding of paws echoed in Granite's triangular ears. He

loved to be on the move. Never before had he been so happy. Though the oreo-collered wolf wasn't sure where he was going, he felt it getting closer. Aqua felt it too. The brothers could see it in each other's eyes. A spark, a glisten, and a promise of something new. Climbing the mountain in ecstasy, the pack sped up the range.

The sun was beginning to come up, dawning on three tired wolves and a human lost in deep sleep. The terrain had leveled off a bit, as they were no longer diagonally climbing for altitude. Barely below timberline, Risk caught a whiff of scent that curled his lips up tight. He slowed, the pack slowed, until they all came to a stop.

Risk flattened his ears, touched his nose to the earth and inhaled. Pulling his head back up he turned back to Granite and Aqua showing them pink gums, flagging foreign territory. The scent was heavy, strong, and fresh. The message was very aggressive, left for intruders and pack mates alike. It said,

"This is my land. Back off! You do not belong here, unless you are of my pack. Brothers, do not forget that I own you! I AM alpha! Beware! I will fight and you *will* die."

Risk snorted the message out of his snout. It was odd, it was evil. Strangest of all, it was left by a bitch.

Lifting a heavy eyelid, Cara blinked into the brightness of the morning sun. The wolves were stopped and shifting uneasily. Risk was looking back at her for direction. Stepping out of the sled, her bones and tendons popped as she stood on the still cold earth. A breath of dew was accumulating on the sparse alpine flowers scattering the land. Walking towards Risk, she could smell wolf territory. The marking was on a tree stump a few feet away and the urine still smelled hot and vinegary.

It was a recent marking, no more than a day old. The yellow eyed wolf at the lead of the team whined high in his nose to Cara. Risk felt uneasy here after reading the marking. If they crossed paths with the she-wolf and her pack, a fight and blood shed would certainly follow. Trying to soothe her wolf, Cara massaged Risk's head, pressing his ears back with each stroke of her palm.

The pack was hungry and tired. The odors emitted from each wolf were smells of an empty body in need of nourishment, bad breath and a shift in musk. Cara wondered if they could rest here. Would they be safe? The wind tossed her hair in curling designs, already wild from sleep. It was not in their favor. If they stayed here the breeze would carry their scent like a letter and alert the native troop.

Treading softly Cara walked about, looking in every direction. They would have to go back half a mile. Just to eat and rest out of she-wolf territory. Still, the wolves would smell them but doubtfully protrude to attack. Nourish the pack first. Then they would be ready to return and cross this wild country. Wolves and all.

After eating a meal of dried game and bread, Cara stashed the remaining food in a tree branch. Cara loved the chore of securing food from the bears because; she loved to climb up in trees. Probably just another little something lingering from her childhood. Although the weather was warm and she was sufficiently fed, Cara was not at ease. She was nervous, and the wolves could sense it.

After arriving at a safe spot, Risk paced back and forth despite his longing to rest. Meanwhile exhaustion swept the two brothers away, leaving them tossing and twitching in their sleep. Coming down from the tree Cara slipped and crashed to the ground with a thud. She landed on her feet and hands, and was mostly unharmed by the mishap. Her fall brought Risk over to her, to lick her cheek and bury his head beneath her arm.

"I will protect you, white river."

Risk often called Cara by many names of endearment. Usually after something beautiful or powerful the two had seen or shared together. Though Risk was growing older and wiser, it still made Cara frown to have him tend to her weaknesses. She was to care for him, to the dogs she had to be seen as alpha. But as time went on, she realized this relationship was far more than any canine hierarchy. These wolves were spirit wolves, comprehending far more than basic survival strategies. They shared a bond made from love, trust and loyalty. She cared for Risk when in need and he was to do the same for her. Her pride could deal with that.

Cara pushed hard to get off the ground, and walked with heavy feet to where the brothers had curled up in the shadow of a fallen tree. Aqua ran wildly in his dreams, kicking Granite twice in the snout. Instead of curling up with Aqua, Cara stretched out upon a slice of earth, between Granite and the log.

Pressing her back flat against the tree, the bark felt cool and soothed her muscles that still tremored in shock. Crossing between his brothers, Risk came to lie in front of Cara and his black brother. Stretching out like a lazy dog on a hot day, he offered his haunch to her as a pillow. After a few deep breaths, they both fell asleep.

The cradle of rest didn't keep any of the wolves for very long. Dark clouds thundered across the sky like buffalo herds on the prairie plains. Ears twitched and sleepy eyes opened until the pack was up.

"I smell rain."

Aqua had put a paw on Cara's knee as she sat cross legged, stretching the kinks out of her back. Cara laughed with bright eyes as her back popped in between the roars of thunder. Giggling, she stoked the neck of the smallest wolf and hugged Aqua close.

"It's on the way, my blue eyes. I believe it brings luck when it comes. I think that maybe, we should travel in the falling water. If it's mild, anyway."

Aqua was now lightly gnawing on Cara's fist. He stopped when Cara mentioned traveling in the rain. He pushed his ears forward; he liked what she just said. Aqua loved water, his name was purely coincidence.

"Yeah, but I don't want to run into these wolves, Cara. I smelled their message. They are big, and fierce."

"How do you know they're not bluffing Aqua?" It was Granite who spoke now. He had trotted over to join in the conversation after a play fight with Risk. Earlier, they had acted out an attack from a strange pack, trying to confuse and outwit each other. Though it was no more than a make believe scenario to test their skills, the romp went well and filled them both with courage. Now that they were done, Granite proceeded to talk with the pack while Risk hung back to sniff the air and pee.

In front of Cara and Aqua, Granite stood tall and smiling. His lip was curled and his teeth were glistening in a fierce smile that could back the toughest opponent down. He was a masculine dark figure with splashes of white that highlighted his bulk and size. Cara had no choice but to return his smile. Granite looked like a warrior, absolutely magnificent

In the background, Risk watched over his pack. He felt the first pats of rain drops on his coat. He knew that the rain brought luck as Cara had said. He was ready to enter the other territory. Risk smiled as his beta did to Aqua, showing a wicked grin with the curl of the lip. The rain felt good, and the time was right to move. With his game face on, he watched the silhouette of his beautiful woman as she stood up and headed to the sled.

****

Sprinting through the alpine country, the rain whipped at the pack's faces. Each blow hit with inspiration, and wild eyes looked deep into the future. A sick greed filled their lungs as they gulped in the wet air charging through their throats. Paws hit hard and heavy and Cara lost herself in the moment. She had smeared mud, blood and berry paint on her face to keep her look fierce. Throwing her head back, letting the drops lash at the supple skin of her throat, she howled. It was a call from deep within her body and soul.

"We come! We are strong! We come! We are ready!"

The Raven people say that we all have a song, that's how we know who we are. Cara sang not only to make noise in the world but in times like now, to alert the creatures of her presence.

As they reached the resident pack's border, their stench crawled up into the deepest cavities of the wolves' noses. Cara caught the scent, it was hard not to. Even to her human nose the musky scent of wolf was rich and seemed to be engrained in everything. It was intimidating, sure, but they did not slow their pace.

Risk led his brothers with stealth and speed with no desire to stop or slow down. Nothing driven from fear, just the desire, the calling from a greater destiny that lay ahead. They were going to get through this. Behind him, Aqua panted in a trance-like rhythm, feeling the love and luck that showered down from the pregnant clouds. Their children brought a much needed softness to the dry air. Granite's ears were cupped and alert, even at this pace. In the distance, under a rumble of thunder, he heard the cry of the she-wolf.

Thunder paused and lightning struck as if summoned by the bitch. Her call was a sound that no wolf had ever made and it made Cara involuntarily shiver. The wolf screamed like a cat, screeched like an owl, and roared like a bear. All this ferocity, all this sound, from one female in the distance. Her call declared her status. The alpha female.

Her howl was echoed by what sounded like a thousand more. Though the echoing howls were weaker, quieter, and far less threatening than hers. How many members of this pack were there? The yipping and number of short howls were concentrated, either a tactic or a very large pack. Though Cara shivered, she was not afraid. Nor did she feel as if she were trespassing. If anything, she glowed with anticipation to meet this wolf who yowled like a woman and declared herself so mighty.

The storm quieted itself to a humble silent misting. In the

atmosphere above, the clouds scattered away with the breeze. They revealed a clear evening sky, stars and moon shining full strength on the land below. The pack's pace had slowed to a trot, by commands of Cara. She wanted to investigate and tour the new country.

Risk did as he was told, but he had a biting desire to pick up the pace and get out as soon as possible. The tactic from the other pack had worked, and he felt their presence through their surge of sound. It seemed odd to the young alpha male was how no sound had come from the pack sense their first call. He could not hear them coming, nor did his nose alert him of their arrival. But he felt it, they were waiting.

Wind played games with its sister earth. Twirling and spiraling across her voluptuous mounds and skinny trails. Wind shifted his direction entirely, and mixed the smells on the horizons. Risk froze. In front of him sat a tall, thick coated, well fed, crimson brown wolf. It appeared larger than Granite, not in bulk but in presence. To Risk, this wolf towered tall and reeked of grainy stone, rotten meat, and the tender scent of dirt and iron.... wolf blood.

The team was still, including Cara. She dare not move, even the breath inside her held still. Motionless, she stood on the pegs at the back of the jig. Granite, Aqua, and Risk held their tails at a neutral position. They indicated neither fear nor aggression; the only message was that of their existence.

The opposing red wolf studied the statues in front of her for a few breaths longer. It could not snatch their scent and for the first time in a long time, did not see fear in their eyes as she stared them down.

Surprisingly to his brother and to himself, Aqua did not as much as quiver. He kept his eyes locked on the fellow predator ahead. Brother wind gasped deeply and the air stood stagnant. In the stillness, the massive red shot its nose up to the sky and opened wide enough to eat up all the stars. It drew in the warmth of the air, and lingered before letting out a mind vexing shriek.

The noise was a complex sounding of hoots, screams, roars, wails and howls, pulled into one mouthful. It was the same sound that they had heard moments before. This was the she wolf in front of them, and she was calling to her pack mates. Bowing her head down to have another drink of air, she seemed to murmur to herself in a deep, raspy growl. When red picked her head up, she tilted it so that only one side of her face was revealed to the trespassers.

Growling still, her better eye narrowed on the intruders. The yellow surrounding her pupil glowed with the intensity of the harshest rays of the sun. Beneath the almond shape holding her eyes, a bloody gash had scabbed over. Behind the crimson beast, sets of eyes began to glow in the forest. Figures formed around the eyes, shapes that can only belong to wolves. This was the entirety of the bitch's pack. Eight strong, healthy, distinctly vicious members were snarling at the pack and their prized alpha human.

Eight
~~~~~~~~~~~~~~~~~~~~

Cara's breathing remained muffled. She felt as if her lungs might explode at any moment. Her chest was tight and her rib cage hugged her lungs. All from the brain's impulse of fear. Her body's guard was up and it was time to act. She side stepped and crouched low to the earth. Spreading her fingers wide she palmed the ground quietly, crawling to Granite's side. Crimson wolf's head did not move to watch the woman move. Instead, the darkest black in her pupil shifted to follow the human's actions.

The sound of the clicking metal and of the pulling loose of rope was muted by the wind's aid of breeze. Her wolves were free from harnesses and could step from the pile of rope without tangle. Hand on Granite's bulky shoulder, Cara bulked herself up and stood every inch of her height.

Although they did not show it, the native wolves saw Cara rise as tall as a grizzly bear, and they were afraid. Fear was not tolerated by the blood red bitch and so, the nearest three wolves jumped the woman and knocked her down. Noise was punched out of Cara when she hit the ground. Not only had she been knocked down, but the warm wetness of blood rolled down her thigh. When the wolves took her down, her hip had dug into a rock and a patch of gravel.

Footsteps away, the she wolf twitched her nose, the most movement that had come from her since her last cry. The wolf was intrigued by the aroma of blood. She would get her taste of it, but for now, instead of engaging in this battle, she'd rather watch.

Risk, Granite and Aqua jetted to Cara's rescue the moment the wolves leaped. Still, one male had time to sink his fangs deep into the tender flesh of the human's calf muscle. Cara howled similarly to the blood-curdling cry of the she-wolf. Utter pain.

At this, the crimson canine was thoroughly amazed. Another creature matching her calls was literally unheard of. But she *had* heard the soft-fleshed creature cry out in a tone far too filled with pain to be mockery or mimic. Springing towards the rabid pile of wolves covering the human, Crimson wolf knocked two of her kin down and bit the haunch of the third.

"MMMIIINNNEEE!!!"

is what the bitten wolf snarled and spat to the alpha female. Obviously, propriety was of no concern to this pack.

"NO!! LET THIS ONE LIVE!"

Crimson wolf strained her voice to spit and growl this command. However, the attacking wolves pulled back into the woods by the time the bitch finished snapping. Spit dripped from her jaws in an ugly snarl that served as warning to both her pack and the invading one. She had no allies.

Granite had taken a blow to the shoulder and Aqua was missing tufts of his coat. Risk was untouched. At Cara's side, Risk lowered his head allowing Cara to wrap her arms around his neck like a crutch. She could not walk and her blood loss was significant. The battlefield went still. Both the wolf's and woman's hearts were pulsing with the moment. The here, the now.

Cara was dragged to her jig where she could pull herself up to stand and seem tall once more. The red wolf paced back and forth. The new blood was toying with her emotions and senses. Yes, she wanted the blood, wanted the taste. But she also wanted to know more of the creature from which the blood was spilled. Then she thought, what of the wolves who followed her? Were they a threat? Certainly the golden eyed gray male did not fear her, which could be bad. What were they doing here? Perhaps what intrigued the she-wolf most of all was the scent of another female.

Cara was hurting, badly. Her leg pulsed as the blood pumped out of her hip and leg. She opened her mouth to speak to the alpha female, but only a gasp of hot, dead oxygen came out as Risk went charging towards Crimson wolf. The two wolves collided with roaring snarls and slashing claws.

Jaws locked, paws on shoulders, each stood on their hind legs.

It looked as if they were dancing a violent waltz. Then Risk lost his footing and stumbled down to the ground, and the red wolf had an advantage. She threw her weight on Risk's neck, forcing his stance to crumble. With the gray wolf howling beneath her chest, she began to bite and rip at his flanks and ribs. The brothers rushed to tear the bitch off their brother.

They were immediately intercepted. A group of four young males greeted their attempts of interruption with roars and flashing canines. The brothers snarled back, and Granite raised his fur to double his size. The young males reacted without hesitation and lunged atop the brothers, and a new battle was underway.

Standing in astonishment, Cara remained untouched. It was as if she had been pardoned from this battle. Fights swirled around her while she was forced to watch from the sideline. Besides, there was little she could do to interfere at this point anyway. Storms of fur and teeth and claws prevented her from getting in the action.

Once Cara clamored back to the sled, she immediately tourniqueted her calf and bandaged the wound on her hip. Her hands shook and her palms were sweaty as she nervously watched and waited to see the outcome of this quarrel. Brain rattling, she assessed every detail possible. Watching gestures, mannerisms and underbellies, Cara realized that of the wolves she had seen, all had been male but the alpha. Either way, Cara chanted and prayed that her pack could make it through this territory alive.

The quarrel between the brothers and the four males raged on. Fangs clattered, gums were bloody and growls made the air heavy. Sliding on his belly, a young male caught Aqua off guard and sunk his teeth into his front leg, hitting bone. With another male snapping at his chest, Aqua's eyes blue eyes turned ice white in fury.

Striking like a rattlesnake, Aqua grabbed the male who bit his leg by the loose fur on his neck. It squealed like a pup and flipped over to reveal his belly in submission. As Aqua lowered his head to receive the wolf's pleas for mercy, the traitor snapped in his face and tore open his nose. Rolling on his belly had been a dirty trick but Aqua's blood sprayed the cheater like a waterfall, getting in his eyes and keeping him from getting out from under Aqua's pin. The plan had backfired for the young male.

On his next breath, he choked on the metallic blood pouring down his throat. The he felt the blue-eyed wolf's fangs slice through his neck, cutting through his jugular veins. With that, his life was taken from him. Aqua had ripped out his throat, and spat it at the young male's brother. In turn the red brother tucked his tale beneath him and darted off into the woods, whining and squealing like a pig.

Killing a wolf in a fight was not something Aqua had ever done, or had planned to do. In the world of the wolf, mercy and humility give the lesser wolf his life. It puts members in rank and keeps the pack strong, aware of its weaknesses.

Aqua glanced over to see Granite's fur matted with blood. A similar situation had obviously occurred to him as well. Granite dueled with the lingering male, exchanging leaps and bounds over the dead body of the third red male. It also had its throat removed, along with numerous other rips in the flesh left from Granite's deadly bite. Aqua sneezed blood and stole Granite's attention. His brother looked savagely deadly and unfamiliar to Aqua. He had never seen this side of his own littermate.

Barking his curses, Granite turned back to the cowering male and threw him aside. He hit the ground with all his weight and lay there still, unconscious. Granite barked Aqua to his side, for his eyes were clouded with anger and he could no longer see Risk. Aqua nudged his brother's muzzle in the direction of where the alphas paced.

Crimson wolf and Risk's tangle occurred simultaneously with Granite and Aqua's fight with the brothers. During that time, each had called the other's move with exceptional accuracy. After much pacing and sizing-up, neither wolf suffered dramatic damage from the duel. The red devil did not submit to Risk and he did not cower to her. Exhausted, they called a bit of a truce.

Back at the sled the brothers and Cara watched as the two alphas circled and sniffed in greeting, instead of in challenge. The Crimson wolf was wooed by the gentle air of Risk and she showed her infatuation with a low moan that came from her own heat. With this, the eighth wolf came racing towards them from out of the shadows. He had remained in the distance as his pack mates were destroyed and defeated.

Racing towards them, he was of dense, compact build and bore traits from horror stories. His fur was a fiery red, though torn out in chunks along his body. The bared skin was scabbed and scarred over thick, rippling muscles. The flesh of his upper lip was missing entirely, leaving him in constant snarl with long fangs hanging outside his mouth. His eyes glowed but revealed no pupil, like the cold eyes of a shark. He was no less than terrifying.

The sun was setting and Cara could not be sure if this new creature would be more frightening revealed in the light or hidden in the upcoming darkness. She hoped she would not have to find out. Something about this fire-coated wolf brought dread deep inside her. It seemed he was followed by a trail of death and the darkest shadows.

The tameness that had revealed itself it the greeting between the bitch and Risk disappeared. A look of dread, worry, and frustration matted the she-wolf's eyes as her mate dispatched from the shadows. Risk felt pity for Crimson wolf; he knew her story in an instant. This male had trapped her into a life of aggression and hate. Risk studied closely as the bitch's dread spiraled to disbelief, to anger, then finalized with sheer fury. She swung her head to meet her mate in a vicious, drooling snarl. She took a bite from the fiery male's belly and caught a mouthful of hair in her jaws. She had been the one stripping his fur and presumably, the cause of his missing lip.

In the growing darkness, Fire wolf and Crimson wolf circled each other. It seemed this was the final duel. Cara's pack retreated to her side, all watching the red wolves' performance. Cara learned much from this face off.

****

The Crimson wolf was named Rage and her mate went by the name Fire. Rage and Fire had been mates for four long years. Fire was three years older than Rage and clearly descending from his prime. Rage had come to this pack as an outcast spirit wolf. Not so much was she an outcast as she was simply left behind, a runt.

Left alone in the harshest of seasons had given Crimson wolf the opportunity to toughen up and fend for herself. The cruel impact of struggle in her life had given Rage an edge at an early age. She was the perfect opponent in Fire's eyes. The difference between the two was that deep down, Rage was loving, tender, and hurt.

Fire found her alone in unclaimed territory, northwest of the mountains. She had resided in the fertile Harvest Valley and was beginning to prosper as a lone wolf. Fire watched her for days as she hunted, slept and grew up alone, in exile.

The red wolf seized the opportunity that lingered below and took the female back to his own lands. On the way, they had fought to near death multiple times. The wars only halted when things like hunger or exhaustion got in the way. Rage did not want to go to his barren lands; Fire would not allow her to return. It seemed like a curse to Rage when she woke beside her red companion. Often he was beaten to the core and she, equally bloody and very alone.

Her life with Fire began the moment she arrived to his territory. He mounted her in front of his pack of three envious males, and then took off on a hunt. Full with Fire's fuel, Rage longed for a female to guide her and help her understand. She would search for company on days she was forced to scout out denning locations. The only female wolf Rage ever found was an old, dying outlier. The old female sniffed Rage in greeting, and told her many stories of her life and Rage's captor and mate.

The old bag of organs said that she had mothered Fire as punishment from invading the spirit worlds. Her pup was something to beware of, all that surrounded him was said to spiral into darkness. And so, Rage spoke with Fire's mother, Flame, for days at a time. She became a maternal figure to Rage and it eased her through her pregnancy with the spawn of the demon dog.

Flame explained that after the birth of Fire, she never had another fertile litter. Another curse, as it was made to seem, was that Fire could sire only male pups, as stir-crazed and filled with blood lust as he. He would take a mate and kill her after she produced soldiers for his army. Rage would have to become lethal if she wanted to survive.

Nightly after the female's meetings, the weary wolf would howl in sorrow for Rage. Calling for mercy on her and apologizing to the spirit worlds and begging to rid the earth of her curse. One evening, Fire heard his mother's voice in the distance. He was not pleased.

The next morning Rage went to seek Flame's advice once more. She came to find the old wolf dead, her throat ripped out and all. It was the work of Fire, unpredictable and wild. Alone Rage returned to her empty den with a basket full of puppies and a heart full of sorrow.

****

All of this past, the two red wolves circled, ready to duel. Rage hated Fire from the moment they met. Looking into his eerie eyes she saw what she hated most, and what she was familiar with; anger, aggression and vacant nothingness.

Rage did not cock her head back when she let out this howl.

Instead, with her eyes locked on Fire, she screamed. She cried to the spirit worlds as Flame once had, for mercy and apology, then she altered her tune into a hissing whine. Rage made sounds that were different from her previous howling shrieks. None the less, her sound drew blood from the ears of her own mate. It was painful.

Legend has it that there is a serpent inside of us all. The serpent is only stirred by great emotion and anger, only then does it speak. This was the serpent's hiss from her belly, and it snaked and spiraled in the red of her eyes. A deep hurt fueled Rage's launch towards Fire. She hit him with so much force he was knocked off his feet and ate dirt. With Fire on his side, Crimson wolf began tearing chunks of flesh and fur from Fire's flank. Blood sprayed everywhere.

Fire retaliated by grabbing the soft flesh of her underbelly, stealing her balance and pulling her to the same earth that he lay upon. Rage yelped like a pup from the bite, equally shocked by the attack as well as from the red life flowing from the break in her skin. Fire picked his mate up by the scruff of her collar and shook her like a rag, back and forth, violently. He dropped her when she cried out and begged for mercy. Drooling and spitting Fire nosed her to her feet, nipping at her paws until she stood. He wasn't finished with her. Showing signs of weakness, Rage waited for her next attack, she knew this game. Fire fell for her disguise and pinned her once more. He went for her throat.

Intercepted.

Granite had taken a stand. It was not in his nature to watch such immoral bloodshed. He too could see the hurt and abuse oozing from Rage. She had surrendered and her mate disregarded her request for life. That show made Fire weak. The strong accept mercy and move on. This one did not.

There was something about the Crimson wolf that appealed to Granite and because of this; he chose to fight for the she-wolf's survival. He had also seen her spare the life of his human pack mate. That deed alone was enough to spare her life from the blood thirsty mutt of mass destruction. So, when Fire pulled back as a hawk does before it strikes, Granite seized the moment and rammed into him with the force of ten wolves charging.

A new fight had begun and in short, Granite was loosing. Rage rushed to his aid but was ripped open in the throat instead. She could do nothing. Blood loss and lack of food forced the bitch to crumple unconscious in a puddle of her own blood and vomit. Aqua had also come to the aid of his brother but he was repelled by the deadly snapping jaws of the red male. Blood was spilled from both competitors and Aqua was thrown against a dense tree stump, resulting in his leaving the conscious world.

Granite was significantly bloody from his tackle fight with Fire. Risk watched his beta male duel from the relative safety of the sled. Cara was too wounded to fend for herself properly and he was her last line of defense if matters came to their worst. The woman could not even shoot off an arrow for she feared that it would turn the raging bull of a wolf towards her. She could become his new target and without Risk to protect her in this state, she would surely die.

Fire was getting tired, it was showing. Not in the teasing illusionary way that his pack mates had looked tired, but his blood loss was excessive and his eyes were dull from weeks of hunger. Granite's limbs shook with depletion, but he could take this demon down. He was a spirit wolf, and this red male was bad, very bad. He could see and smell it.

She-wolf good, red male wolf bad. That thought echoed in his mind and began ringing in his ears with each heart beat. His father and his mother would not like this wolf. It threatened Cara, it threatened the pack. Now, riddance of the devil was his new task. Granite was indeed a warrior.

Two attacks.

One dash and granite tore off Fire's previously bloody ear. Next, a crushing bite on the snout. To Granite's surprise when he locked onto Fire's hideously disfigured muzzle, it crumbled under his jaws like the kibbles Cara gave him.

Fire shrieked with the chilling sound as his mate once made. Blood was flowing from everywhere. Jagged chunks of cartilage had erupted from beneath his skin. Standing tall and watching the demon spew and vomit uncontrollably, Granite knew that he had won. The battle was over. The darkness was spewing out of his opponent and when that was out, his vessel of a body would atrophy. Fire would die by morning.

The evil male with the hollow eyes and never ending snarl gave one last fierce glare to the remaining wolves and human. He had not stopped shrieking as he studied his reapers. Fire did not tuck his tail beneath him when he turned to leave, he only ran. He disappeared into the woods from which he had come, leaving a trail of blood along the way.

Nine

~~~~~~~~~~~~~~~~~~~~~~~~~~~~~~~

Cara called for Granite through a choked sob. She embraced the
wolf with open arms and let her tears dampen his oreo-colered coat.
He smelled rancid, but Cara did not care. Risk nuzzled his brother as
Cara continued her weeping embrace. Risk showed worry in his
yellow wolf eyes. He too, had feared the loss of his family.

The tearful wolf woman reluctantly released Granite. The awful
cries from the forest had not yet stopped. If anything, they had
intensified. They weren't coming closer, they weren't getting more
distant, and they came from the same spot, louder and creepier than
before.

Cara rested her elbows on her knees and hung her head
between her legs, cradling it with her hands. Plugging her ears and
shutting her eyes she wanted all this to go away. Risk pressed close to
her to remind her than she was no longer in danger, he would keep
her safe. Granite's tongue caressed her leg, cleaning the blood spilling
from the bandage. She forced herself to open her eyes and take
charge. There was still Aqua and the Crimson wolf to deal with.

As she pulled herself up to stand, Cara studied the broken
tree limbs, cracked boulders, and blood stains on the pale. loose dirt.
Holding on to the shoulders of Risk and Granite, Cara limped to the
fist recognizable corpse. Crimson wolf. The scene was sickening and
the smell pulled the remaining supper from Cara's stomach.

Bending down to feel the breath pushing up Rage's ribs, the she
wolf opened one eye to inspect her saviors. Seeing it wasn't another
red wolf, she shut her eye and let her body go limp. Cara asked
Granite to drag Rage closer to the jig. Cara wanted to save her, seeing
a potential friend and pack mate. Granite gladly obeyed and gently
pulled her body away.

After crossing two red wolf corpses, they found Aqua. Risk
woke him up by whining softly into his ear.

"How badly are you hurt brother?"

After hacking and snorting dirt and blood from his nose Aqua
replied,

"At least now I'm breathing, I think..."

He stood on four shaky legs.

"Look Cara. I'm standing too."

Aqua looked around and sniffed. Ears pricking, he locked onto Fire's howling in the distance. Aqua did not ask about the shrieking and moaning in the distance. Cara knew her brother was in bad shape but the pack was in a bad place, so she had to ask,

"My blue eyes, can you run for me? I want to get out of this place. As you can see, I'm badly hurt."

Aqua nodded to Cara and loped off to the jig and pile of harnesses.

"Let's go."

He waited as Cara hobbled back to hook him and his brothers up to the sleigh. His curiosity was killing him so at last Aqua asked,

"Why does Fire continue to cry so? Will he not die?"

The answering silence kept him quiet for the rest of the evening.

Cara pulled Rage's body onto the jig, straining her muscles and cursing with each move. Cara forced herself to stand on the pegs at the back of the jig. Her knees tried to give out and the whooshing of blood from her brain to her calf almost drowned out the shrill sounds from the woods. One last look at the dead wolves and bloodied land was enough to make her swallow her pain.

Risk took off, pulling most of the weight for his wounded partners. Cara watched as the bloodied scene faded away into the darkness. For the first time in a long time, she had truly been afraid.

With each bump of the jig, Cara winced in pain. Her injuries were much worse than she had initially thought. Their continual bleeding made her increasingly nervous for her health. That was only the first problem of the moment. Watching the pack pull her and the Crimson wolf, she could see that each member was straining to pull and run. They were all trying so hard, trying for her, because they knew she was not safe. A moment of guilt passed by, and Cara pondered if she made her family happy.

Third problem, she felt she had gotten them all into this situation with the red wolves. It was as if she had bruised and bloodied the pack herself. She insisted they press on, she didn't think they were destructible. She was wrong and almost lost her family because of her ignorance. Guilt, blame, conflict and responsibility. She had to stop and accept things were out of her control.

Breathing in deeply, Cara buried her thoughts and brought

herself back to the moment. Indeed her whirling thoughts had gotten the better of her, for now she realized the remarkable distance the wolves had covered in such short time. Or had it been a long time? Her own pulsing beat could easily have sent her into a trance. Looking ahead she could see Risk's chest expanding and contracting as he gulped up as much air as his lungs would allow. He was pulling far more weight than usual and though he showed no signs of slowing, Cara knew it was time to stop. Risk would die before he gave up.

They had arrived at a point where trees and grass resumed their growth. The altitude had gone down and full bodied trees and bushes replaced the previous scenery of stumps, dirt and alpine boulders. There wasn't any fresh water around yet, but the canteen was full and her reserve keg stocked as well. As the wolves waited to be freed, they stood with their legs stiff and heads down, like exhausted cattle on the Oregon trail.

With snaps and clinks of metal the wolves were freed from their harness. The crimson wolf remained unconscious from exhaustion. While Cara readied some food for the wolves, Granite dragged Rage off of the sled by the thick fur on her neck. He toted her to a spot beneath a hanging maple tree and waited.

Risk wanted to hunt but was fiercely denied, with glares and snarls in response. Tough love. Cara would not have it. She insisted on inspecting each wolf and attending to all wounds before attending to her own any further. With a huff of disappointment, Risk went off to further inspect the sleeping grounds and ensure safety for the pack.

A gift from the tiger, Cara had skills in healing. In the back of her mind, she prayed that they would be of service tonight. First, food and water was presented for the pack. Aqua drank with such enthusiasm that Cara had to scold him to prevent him from throwing up. Dried slices of moose was what made up the menu and the diners gulped it up with relative ease and grateful satisfaction. Risk and Granite disappeared after their meal to continue their previous activities while Cara readied to play doctor.

Aqua was the first inspected. He lay still as human fingers stroked, poked, and pressed his body. The soft touch of naked flesh explored all his wolfy body, searching for injury. His bleeding had slowed if not stopped and all sources of blood were nothing but breaks in the flesh. The most damage done was internal, but he would heal. Another night perhaps Cara could tend to those wounds as well.

For now, she prescribed Aqua to sleep by her side as soon as she finished looking over the others. Aqua knew the comfort of another's body eased the pain of any injury and Cara's body gave him a sense of security, even in knowing she was around. Aqua lowered his muzzle to the ground and shut his eyes in wait. The shrieking in the distance had not stopped although now, one had to strain to hear it. That was good enough. With one final sigh, Aqua got a head start on his orders and fell into a deep, healing sleep while Cara busied herself with the rest of the pack.

Granite stood guard over Rage though no matter how intensely he watched her red-furred body rise and fall, the Crimson wolf lay still in her sleep. A mild nose twitch was all the effort she cared to exert when the dry meat was presented for her. Though Rage was motionless, it was hard to pull Granite away. With reasonable force and intimidation, Cara grounded Granite so that she could care for him. With the blood soaked beta beneath her, whining and squirming, Cara began her study. She found no broken bones or torn arteries. Mostly blood from other wolves. The smell was foul. A tooth was cracked and Granite's ear was torn but Cara mended it together with a rather precise stitch. With that, Granite followed at Cara's heels as she approached the sleeping Rage.

Blood was trickling from a cut inside Rage's mouth; it was beginning to make a shallow pool of blood beneath her chin. Caution, hesitation, and reluctance acted as signals to her brain to stay away but her loves of the wolf made Cara come to Rage's aid. The wolf slept heavily as if she were drugged. Cara was able to lift Rage's jaw without her even opening an eye. Granite, practically looking over Cara's shoulder, pawed the ground nervously.

When Cara lifted her patient's lips to find the source of the blood, Rage snarled and snapped blindly, still asleep. Cara felt a flash of pain. Rage's tooth snagged the fragile flesh of the woman's hand. When her blood danced out in a wavering curl, Rage sniffed, opened one eye, and licked the wound. Relaxing her body, Cara went in to troubleshoot the wolf's mouth once more.

This time, Rage was still. Her breathing remained easy and her tail even thumped once out of subconscious thanks when Cara rubbed sage on her infected, freshly wounded gums. Cara was less thorough on the body of the Crimson wolf, but from what she could tell, she was fine. With Granite's approval, Cara hobbled back to the sled to meet Risk. Granite did not follow. Exhausted but wrapped up in an awkward calm, Granite curled up beside the red wolf. Their touching furs warmed him deep inside, and cradled him to sleep.

At this point, the pain was unbearable. Cara collapsed gracelessly beside the jig. Fast to her side, Risk licked her cheek and tasted a salty tear. The day had been too hard on the woman and the night had been no kinder. At least now, it was all over. Risk turned to show Cara the side of his body that had been mauled by Rage earlier in the evening. Bites and missing chunks of fur gave him an aging character. He had hidden his body from her before but now Cara could see it was nothing to worry over. The wolf would heal, he was strong.

Risk stepped one foot over his lady and let her breathe into his wide, furried chest. Looking up to the night sky, Risk cried a silent howl that made a puff of steam in the air. Beneath him, Cara's sobs of pain rattled through his chest cavity. She was too tired to heal herself. She had to expel the wounding emotions of fear and sorrow through a cleansing sob. Letting her cry, Risk stepped back to her side and sprawled out beside her. Whining only to her, sharing pain and exhaustion, he let her curl her fingers into his fur and pull him close, pressing against the shapes of her body. With his tail as their blanket, they fell asleep under the wide sky and shining stars.

****

The dawning of a new day brought the pack safety and relief. They were no longer in Fire's territory, and so all seemed to settle to calm. Rage's eyes were the first to open and take in the sweet yellow sunshine. Yawning wide, Rage's head throbbed and her senses felt dull. She tried to stand but, her muscles quivered and refused. Exhaling impatiently, Rage viewed the defined steely muscles in her forearms as nothing more than useless strips of meat. They felt like jerky, dry and stiff.

Looking around, Rage's new arrangement slammed into her like a rough tidal wave off the Alaskan coast. She remembered last night; she remembered the fight and all the terrible pain Fire put her through. Rage snorted in disgust. That was all over now.

Her focus quickly shifted to the naked pile of flesh curled beside the foreign pack's alpha wolf. He was the one who held a face off with her and showed no fear. Was that female thing next to him his mate? Whatever the creature was, Rage had not seen anything like her before. Perhaps she recalled something similar from her ever-hazy memories of the spirit world, but nothing came to mind. Not like this, never had she seen anything so real and alive.

The fleshy female's eyes burst open as if from the pressure of Rage's intense studying stare. When their eyes met, Rage felt as if she had been hugged and healed. There was a certain amount of trust the woman had in her, yet she could not understand why such a foreign creature would have this. Locked in a gaze with Cara, Rage once again saw no fear.

The handsome wolf beside the skin-bitch lifted his head. His cause for awakening was no doubt the slight movement from his partner. Rage envied the relationship she saw unfolding before her. How it was that a female had such power and strength without bitter ferocity? It inspired her. Suddenly, Rage felt like a runt pup in the den, longing to join in with the others, feel the joy of companionship and feel the strength of the pack.

Looking at Rage, Cara could see the emptiness in the bitch's almond shaped, mustard colored eyes. The anger and violence that had streaked Rage's eyes red had vanished. With that shattered, an invisible sun seemed to glow inside her and light up her gaze. Watching the Crimson wolf study her, Cara felt flattered. She knew she was envied by Rage.

It was warm in the morning. The wolves had all slept for many hours, allowing their bodies to heal. To further their progress in the healing cycle, food and water was next in store. Cara ruffled Risk's coat and came across a dried patch of blood in his fur. His blood reminded her of her own and as she looked at her swollen leg. It seemed as if her limb belonged to a stranger. It was too bruised and inflamed to be hers. The only confirming identification was the leather band aid that she had applied last night. Now it was soaked in layers of her own drying blood. Turning to Risk, Cara began to speak at the same moment he did. They said in unison,

"We need to find water".

However Risk inferred that *he* had to find water, knowing Cara was in no shape to go exploring. Risk flattened his ears to her, hoping his comment had not been too dominate of an implication to her. He didn't mean to embarrass her for he knew she could hardly even move. Risk did not want to push her just so she could prove a point. Alphas are to never appear weak in front of their pack. Regardless the circumstance. Cara was no different. However, she did not take offense. She liked to see Risk's strength as a mother does her child's success. She only laughed when Risk submitted like a pup.

"Ok puppy, go find water where we can drink and I can bathe safely. Howl to us what you find. I'll stay and care for the others. Hunt on your way for you are the healthiest one here and we could use your strength."

A grateful smile stretched Cara's lips and Risk panted his gratitude to be of such value to her. He got immense pleasure from pleasing her. After throwing his muzzle beneath her chin, Risk was off to the west, where the mountains began to die. Risk's hurried departure woke Granite, though he did not rise. Aqua however slept still, in peace.

Groaning, all Cara wanted to do was sleep. Her eyelids sagged heavily and her wounds screamed at her when she tried to stand. Her brain screamed at her to get up and obey the pulling at her spirit. It had gotten stronger and seemed to add a new kind of pain into the equation. Rising, Cara felt her knees lock to prevent a fall. The power of her heart had silenced the screaming pain as her body focused. Seeing Cara standing she seemed strong and unharmed by last night's near-death. Granite revealed a bit of his own weakness through a limp as he came to her. He wanted her to heal him, and he liked her palm. The pink tongue that dabbed wetness on Cara's open palm was warm and soft.

With confidence in Risk out on the hunt, Cara fed the wolves generously from the food reserve on the jig. She too ate as much as her basket could hold. Aqua awoke from the noise of her stirring. His eyes were clear and he was on a fast track to the road of recovery. Tail swishing, he wanted to take off and join Risk on the hunt. Granite shut him down with a mouthing on his muzzle. After lapping up stale water from a cloth dish, Aqua settled for another nap at Cara's side.

Meanwhile, Rage remained motionless in the spot she had been dropped off at. Her limbs were not broken, just sore. Either way Rage rested there, eyeballing Cara's every move with equal amounts of jealousy and respect. Bringing food and drink, the broken woman hobbled over to Rage very cautiously. When Rage gazed into her eyes, she did not look away. This woman was not afraid, and her strength shone like a white ball of healing light. She seemed to ignore the drizzling of blood coming fro her leg. It was as if the fleshy thing was immune to fear and pain. All the more amazing.

Though she made no effort to get up, Rage was thrilled to taste the dry meat and drink the canteen flavored water left by Cara. The pungent taste of sage had thickened in her sleep. The medicinal herb had tainted her saliva but her mouth ached less. For that, Rage was grateful. In all her time around the new pack, Rage had not yet uttered a word or sound to anyone. In addition, her movements had been minimal as well as her eye contact. She was letting her rescuers know very little about her, her mood, and her health. It was a survival technique, not insecurity. Or at least, that what Rage imagined it to be.

****

The next couple of days passed by like grains of sand, sifting through time's fingers. The pack was healing. Risk's hunts were always successful and he provided enough food to eat for the entire pack. After the second day of resting, Rage left the group to go and hunt for herself. She had still not spoken to anyone, yet she snuck glances of them as often as she could. Rage was fascinated with the pack but dare not let them know. She did not want to be taken advantage of again.

After Rage's departure, Cara wondered if she would return. Why would she come back? Where else would the she-wolf go? Was Rage upset with the pack? Was she going to find Fire and attack? Cara doubted the last. But as usual, the endless questions haunted her throughout the day. In addition, Cara couldn't push away the feeling that Rage belonged in her pack, and Cara knew that Granite felt the same way. He had been guarding her and attempting to court her from the moment Rage regained consciousness. Cara wondered when she too, would find a love of her own. That night, she thought of Whispering Bill's face

Out on the hunt, Rage's thoughts played music in her mind, echoing the padding of her paws. She had devoured a marmot, the chase was exhilarating and the prey was enough to keep her full. On her way back to the pack's grounds, Rage was still hunting. This time, it was for more than just another meal. Rage hunted for family and a place of belonging. Rage wanted to feel something she had never felt before, something like the love that the old wolf Flame spoke of. Approaching Cara's family, here it was, the love Rage so desperately hunted. It was easy prey that simply presented itself on that bloody night, moons ago. Here was love and acceptance, waiting for her behind the bushes. Rage hesitated; she wasn't ready to go back yet.

She was too vulnerable to their kindness. Rage turned her back on them and trotted back into the night.

Crossing a vaguely familiar valley, a dark figure dashed in the corner of Rage's eye. Turning on a dime, her body followed the motion like a metal to a magnet. A late-born caribou calf spent all of it's energy in one last injured bound. The precautionary movement was that which gave her away. Rage had been too distracted to have even noticed the shaking calf cowering in the shadows. Somehow it had strayed from the heard, or was left behind. Either way, the calf would die.

Strong wolf jaws snapped the fragile neck of the caribou. Tasting the warm blood, breathing in the scent of the deer, Rage was high off of another's life essence. In a gulp of blood and meat, she felt as if she captured it's essence. Such feelings were abstract from the more familiar bloodless and taking of life. Instead of taking it to kill, Rage was absorbing it to live. She wanted the woman to be full like this.

After eating her fill Rage realized she was ready to talk. She wanted to run with this pack. Using her newly acquired energy, she dragged the carcass across the hills. The calf was to be a gift to her new family, to prove she could contribute to the strength of the family. Crimson wolf picked up her pace on the way back. It was time to introduce herself and beg for acceptance. She couldn't wait.

Rage's gift was welcomed with open jaws. Like hungry pups, Aqua and Granite fought over the corpse, growling the other into submission and stealing a bite while the other wasn't looking. Jaws snapping wildly, Granite rolled Aqua onto the ground, making him reveal belly. Granite snuffed hot breath at his brother in hungry disgust. The game was over and Granite was ready to eat. Licking his chops and whimpering, Aqua watched his brother devour the remains of the calf. What an alpha would do is go off on another hunt. However, Aqua was happy enough to wait for leftovers. Every member has their place.

Rage spent the remainder of that night talking with Cara. Risk sat at the woman's side for the duration of the entire conversation. His stance looked relaxed and careless but his eyes were focused, intense with guard. He was there as Cara's protection and he was sure Rage knew that.

To Cara, it seemed she and the bitch were equals. She had saved her life, and Rage had spared hers. After hours of learning about the other, Cara accepted Rage into their pack. The food and medical treatment may have seemed as an invitation but truth be told, Cara's curiosity was all that had kept Rage alive up to this point. After their meeting, Cara discovered that the red she-wolf had a soul as wild and untamed as her own. Rage's grave ferocity, unseeing loyalty and power mirrored that of her own and it only made sense to invite her along.

Rage did not pull the sled, but she agreed to learn. Only time and devotion would further her privileges in the pack. Until then, Rage would serve as a scout and a hunter as the pack proceeded on their way to Harvest valley.

Cara raised her head to howl and a booming voice rose from her belly and exited her mouth. The cry seemed to echo for miles. Risk followed her lead, raising the tip of his nose to the sky and singing. Granite and Aqua joined in, cradling the sound of their Alphas. Cara grinned at Rage, a smile that showed her own pointy teeth. Rage wagged her tail, shot her head up and howled a soft, cool note. Nothing like the shriek she had once emitted. Her call mimicked Cara's, and their voices completed the song of the pack.

Ten
~~~~~~~~~~~~~~~~~~~~~~~~~~~~

It was the final leg of the Sedalia pack's journey to the Harvest valley. The terrain was turning mild, hills were hardly steep and there was but one final slope left to summit. Otherwise, the course seemed obstacle free. The pack followed a grizzly's path across the shortening mountains. The trail the bear created was narrow, characterized by trampled moss, turned up earth and flattened soft ground. The jig had no difficulties rolling over it and the wolves ran with such ease that their paws seemed to glide across the lichen and gravel.

In midst of their travels, Cara had to stop the team and bring the sled to a stop. Beside the broken path, Cara had found something that caught her eye. To her left, the ground was untouched. To her right, just beside the trail, Cara saw a set of foot prints. They were side by side, as if the creature was standing in a bi-ped fashion. Cara studied the prints for a long while. So long in fact, that Rage came to her side in impatient protest.

"They are just bear prints. Lets go."

"But these don't look like bear prints, Rage."

Cara pulled her foot from the deerskin boot she wore. She pressed firmly into the mushy ground, beside the prints of the bear.

"See how small these prints are? They almost look like mine, No claws, and round little pads."

"Such a poor design for a predator"

Rage snickered. Cara sighed and shook her head, long hair swaying with her movements.

"These prints just look human, Rage. That's all. Maybe we'll see more."

Before Cara got back on her feet, Rage came to her side and sniffed the prints. They smelled of bear.

Further on down the trail, Cara found more of the same prints. This set however, had inch-deep indentations above each toe pad and they were larger. Clearly, Kodiak prints. Cara couldn't argue this set with Rage or herself. The bear that traveled this trail had been standing tall throughout his journey, searching and smelling. Completely common but, whatever the earlier set of tracks had been they vanished. The rest of the way, there was nothing but bear prints. It seemed somewhat odd, Cara thought. The wolves dismissed it. They were more concerned with how fresh the tracks were, and how heavily the trail smelled of bear. A Kodiak's sense of smell is strong enough to smell a human over two miles away and from the direction of his prints, it would be downwind. Cara hoped the bear had no history like the wolves of this region, and carried on.

An early dawn fell upon the pack the next day. They had been feasting and resting at the base of the final slope, still following the bear's broken trail. It seemed to start and stop sporadically, as if the animal just vanished for a mile or two at a time. Through all the suspicious signs, the pack reminded themselves that they were o the borders of the Spirit lands. As long as they kept their directions true, there was little to worry about. The distorted sights and sounds could be little more than a game being played by the spirits themselves. Despite this, they had made it safely and in high spirits, cocky enough to play games of their own.

The sun woke each wolf by pulling at the tips of every hair on their bodies. The sun made their bodies tingle and urged them all to rise. Cara woke from her sleep to find herself next to her beloved Risk, equally warm and cozy. The itch inside her belly felt like a ring of fire around her navel, and it made her want to play. Cara gave Risk a shot in the shoulder and began a tumbling romp with him.

The rest of the wolves took their time. Stretching their limbs and reaching out with their tongues when they yawned, the pack turned "wake up" into a game. Rage tried to taste the sun, yawning as wide as possible, Granite taunted his brother, rising and luring Aqua to his side to play. When Aqua arrived, Granite would collapse and kick his own paws into the air. Aqua would sneeze in confusion and bark until Granite got up again. The pack mingled and played like this into the heat of the morning until Cara pulled Risk and Rage aside to tell them of her dreams from last night. Aqua and Granite were too involved wiggling on their backs and throwing their paws swimming into the air to be disturbed. Cara readied herself; she was prepared to present her dream.

"I dreamed of Whispering Bill last night, well sort of. I don't know what it means, but at first, I saw myself running fast in a hot dusty valley. My feet, I couldn't see them but I felt them hit the land and they sounded like paws or hooves, in a four-stomp pattern. The ground was hard and my paws slapped with each stride. But I was running. I could smell my hot sweat trickle down my face as I kept up my pace. Running, speeding like a land hawk, through some hot desert."

After seeing that Risk and Rage were still listening with undivided attention and honest intrigue, Cara kept on. She knew her family would not judge her like a human pack would. Dreams were something sacred, and the wolves were fascinated be Cara's.

"So then, I look over to my right and I see something. I still don't know how to describe what it was. It was the image of a bear, a grizzly probably like the one whose trail we've been following. But though I see a galloping bear, I know it is a man and soon, I am running beside him. He does not come after me. Instead we run, neck and neck into a shady canyon leading to an oasis valley. It the valley, we stop and drink at the flowing river. When I look up after quenching my thirst with the cool river water, he is gone. Just, gone. As if he was never even there in the first place. But I look down, and then I see foot prints. They start off as bear tracks, five clawed toes in the sand. Then it looks like the bear stood up for a moment, leaving the deepest prints yet. A foot away, there are the tracks of a man. Five toes, no claws. It is then that I feel my body shift upright, my spine cracking and relocating itself for my human shape. I feel my hands stretch out, and claws retract to nails. I look down and see no fur, only the naked, fragile skin I was born in. So I keep on walking through the oasis, looking for the bear-man. I hear hooves again and I think now, that the padding of my feet I heard was echoed by those of hoofed feet off in the distance. Because I hear the hooves again. I turn to locate the sound. I see nothing. Then, an owl flew down to me and perched on a nearby piece of driftwood. His pupils were no more than specs, and he was tiny. A screech owl I'm guessing and he said to me, there in the broad daylight, that Bill is waiting. And then I woke up."

Rage patted the ground with her tail. Cara had told her of her meeting with Bill, and her growing infatuation. Cara blamed much of it on her overall lack of human companionship that one particular human should seem so special. Rage just lulled her tongue in response. Meanwhile, Risk had been scowling through the intensity of Cara's dream. He too, wondered what it meant. Though he didn't have much experience with interpreting dreams, perhaps it was his spirit heritage that allowed secret meanings to reveal themselves so willingly for him. This dream though, was all to easy. It was naked, with meanings obvious through symbolisms and events.

Cara shrugged off her dream and it's supposed hidden meanings when Granite and Aqua dashed to join the pack in their gathering. It wasn't so much that she didn't want the brothers to hear her night visions as it was how the wind shifted and brought a scent of change on the breeze. It was time for them to get moving. The fire around her navel blazed.

Up hills, down slopes, across flat plains and narrow binds, the pack traveled at a speedy pace. The silent calling, the pulling, picked up their paws as Rage howled back reports of the nearing valley. Cara's heart pumped with anticipation. Her face was flushed, and she sang aloud to the cooling air.

It was nearing sunset when Cara watched the Crimson wolf shoot off into the distance at the speed of a rocket falcon. A trail of dust and pebble was kicked up behind her and soon her bobbing red tail faded away completely into oblivion. Cara didn't worry, and the pack kept on at their steady pace. Whatever Rage went off after, she would report back.

As the bittersweet departure of the sun drew closer, Cara strained to hear a report from Rage. Nothing. Until at last, Cara saw her at the top of the tallest slope, a bit ahead. The figure of Cara's new found companion was filling out nicely sense she'd been living with the pack. And her coat made her easily identifiable. Cara howled to

Rage, letting her know she saw her and that they were on their way. After letting out her wail, the running wolves echoed the message, throwing in some comments of their own.

Rage sat still waiting for her family. She dare not howl back in fear of disrupting the cyclical beauty occurring beneath her. For the first time, Rage was seeing beauty and feeling as if he was a part of it. Slowly, Rage turned her head to peer down at the jig coming up the hill, carrying goods, her new brothers and the heroic human. Rage yawned and sneezed out the dead air. Stretching to stand, she waited for the pack's arrival. She was ready to show them their new home.

****

The pleasure Cara felt from seeing the flourishing sanctuary, the Harvest valley beneath them, gave her such a rush that she was forced to close her eyes and inhale it. Much like a smoker would their cigar, the sensation was overpowering. It was the finest sight she had seen in all her years. Beneath her, the valley was alive in every corner. It was lush and green, with splitters of color from wild bushes and flowers. Freckles of blue and violet gave the seas of green a charming character.

To the west, a rapid river flowed down from a range of mountains that made up the back bone of the valley. The rocky formations stretched to reach the sky, ending in points and plateaus. The river trickled between two flat plateaus that cradled its falling waters into a delicate waterfall. From the hills, the sparkling river ran through a dense pine forest and out into a meadow where a few caribou drank.

Across the field, a heard of horses were crossing the valley, returning to a finely fenced stable. Their coats shone in shades of white, tan, brown, grey, blue and black. The swirls and shades of color that detailed their equine bodies were breathtaking, like nothing Cara had ever seen before. They were stunning creatures, even to the wolves. Foals whinnied and galloped while waiting for the returning members of their herd. And so it was that the pack watched as the heard moved, looking like toy figurines in the distance the horses returned to their stable.

Attached to the stable was a barn, tall and made of stacked

wood. Beside the barn was a small cabin, smoke was rising from a chimney and it seemed to be the nucleus of activity. There seemed to be a buzz of life and Cara scanned the dwelling for signs of life. She could feel the energy from where he was on the hill. It seemed funny how such a small spec of creation conducted so much life and motion. But where was the dweller? Cara continued to look amongst the horses and in between the caribou, searching for a human. She saw nothing until she looked back at the cabin.

Though the cabin was small, it was well designed and even had a wrap around patio. Cara presumed it was established to allow the resident to see at all angles and protect their home, not to mention the incredible view. By the front door, Car spied a flicker of movement. And then, she saw him.

It was the most beautiful sight Cara Sedalia had ever seen, the sparkling jewel of the valley. It was the real reason she had traveled so far. Beneath her, there stood a man on the porch, watching his horses and puffing on a long wooden pipe. He was clearly unaware of how his every movement, even the subtle rise and fall of his chest, dazzled the eyes of the feral woman atop the hill. To Cara, he looked like the character in every romance novel she had ever read. The type of male creation that forced the very author to fall in love with. Every detail was bliss.

The wind picked up and playfully ruffled the long hair of the cabin dweller below. To entertain himself further, brother wind rose up to tickle Cara's nose until she caught the sent of the man below. Grinning, she felt her spine tingle. She recognized the smell from below. It was like rugged earth and fire and stirred her soul like only the most passionate of wolf songs could do. Cara sensed the wolves laughing at her. Never before had she been in such an eager, hungry state. She laughed and said aloud,

"It's not nice to pick on your little sister, wind. Go play with someone else for now, I'm busy."

Up above, the sky was dimming. The man went inside, only to return with a burning oil candle. Cara watched his every movement like a hawk, she was fascinated. He placed the candle on a stand beside a wooden swing. All pieces of furniture were superbly crafted. He lit up a pipe, inhaling in the glow of the candle. He was praying, and waiting for the stars to reveal themselves and dance the night away before him. Cara's eyes reached to see more, but her human tricks failed her in the darkening night, and she could decipher no more. She moved to get a better look but as she stood, the man's eyes grabbed her and made her freeze.

A fire ignited in the cavity of Cara's chest and it began to burn her blood, turning it hot and causing her heart to hammer throughout her rib cage. For a moment she felt like a hiding rabbit that had just been spotted, eyes wide and feet ready to spring. Her heart was thudding away when all of a sudden, she met the eyes of her predator and it stopped. Remembering to breathe, Cara recognized Whispering Bill and smiled.

Wolves and sled behind her, knee still aching and in pain, she rushed down the hill to the valley. The man sitting on the porch rose to take in the sight unfolding before him. His shoulders broad, his gait heavy yet poised, Bill jogged off the porch into the lush fields of green. He stopped as Cara began to near and he opened his arms prepared to embrace her. He on the verge of tears and internal combustion. Cara Sedalia, the woman of his very own dreams and endless fantasies, had finally come to him. All was right in the world. All was right, in that moment.

The love that had blossomed between the two had grown like weeds, even without water. Though only having spent a drop of time together, it watered the vines of love in their hearts and bonded them together. The vines stretched through distances and time to pull the two together, allowing a rich flower to bloom and seal their fate. The flower of love.

His eyes reflected her soul. Wild and fierce, yet caring and gentle he mirrored her. A swirl of colors illuminated his eyes with the same golden shimmer that streaked the colors of her own. In fact, it was his eyes that captured her and swallowed her whole. In them, she could see anything, while leaving everything else behind. His eyes wrapped her heart in an embrace, and it warmed her more than even the thickest bison hide.

For an eternity they stood there, out in the chilling air, lost in each other's arms. The wolves stood waiting in the distance. The embrace shared between Cara and Bill bonded their souls, thoughts, and every little dream and vision from the past. It was all real now; they wee free to create all that was once imagined. They held each other so close, so tight, as if to fuse their hearts together. Pressing to have their hearts beat as one. To breathe as one. To love as one. To be as one.

As man and woman mingled as one, the wolves drew closer as

did Bill's horses. Curiosity and fascination caused both wolves and horses to circulate like friends. A sweet wind from the spirit world spiraled down into the valley and cycloned around Bill and Cara. In tossed her long dark hair across his face and brought chills to his tan flesh. All in a moment, they were one at last. In the quiet valley night, there was not another sound to be heard for miles. Just the breathing of her mate, in sync with her own breath. Cara had to close her eyes and listen with her heart to understand that this was where she belonged.

The first night in the Harvest valley lingered peacefully amongst all it's inhabitants. The spirit horses walked among the wolves with no fear or threat. The pack did not attack a single hoofed being at the cabin, for they had no desire to. The horses here were like their equals and were anything but a target of prey. Even to Rage. Though indeed she did nip at the hooves and tails of the ponies at play in the rich silvery moonlight. Some temptations were just too irresistible to avoid.

The Valley and Things to Come

Eleven
~~~~~~~~~~~~~~~~~~~~~~~~~~~~

   A moon span had gone by sense Cara and the Sedalia pack had arrived in the valley. On this particular night, the dusk began to shift into a complete darkness as another new moon began to grow. The horses were in the shed, a fire was made outside the cabin and the aroma of smoke and meat filled the cup of land they lived on.
   Bill sang a song as he added logs to the fire, feeding the hungry flames. The wolves were sitting around the fire, watching Bill work and laughing as they saw him sneaking glances at Cara with every opportunity. A few feet away, she was carving up the carcass of a dead colt, preparing it for their dinner. Cara had no issues killing or skinning the spirit foal for dinner but Bill however, showed endless remorse for the baby. He hated using his horses as food, and would do it only when life was no longer a possibility for a herd member.
   In this case, Bill had said the colt was too weak to stand and was left behind by his mother. He was birthed out in the frills, away from water and the barn. When Bill found the new born foal, he was dead. In the valley, there did not seem to be a large number of predators. Since Cara had been there and throughout her many nights exploring, she had seen no bears or wolves. The game flourished but no large predators had discovered the utopia below the hills. It puzzled Cara daily but somehow, she always managed to let it go and forget.
   Death sustains life. As Cara carved off portions of the foal for her wolf family, her own stomach roared at the tender meat that slid so effortlessly off the bone. The blood was a rich red, untainted by disease or famine and saliva began to flood her mouth. Swallowing it away, she knew she would have to wait. For now, it was time to feed her brothers. After blessing the food, Cara got ready for the meal-time mayhem to begin.
   Dinner had become a game of sorts for the pack. Cara would throw a slab of meat into air and the wolves raced, jumped and tackled one another to be the first to catch it. A chunk of meat was flung up into the air. Aqua managed to weave around the clusters of

tongues and tails until he raced ahead of the pack. He grabbed the steak and swallowed the mouthful before anyone could catch him or take it away.

The laughter that erupted from the beautiful wild woman sent chills inside of Whispering Bill. A smile stretched across his face and a swelling, scratching, floating sensation came over him. Watching her throw the bloody remains of the colt to the hungry wolves and doing it with such playful joy, Bill realized how endlessly he loved this woman. This was his mate and this was his love. She had the spirit of the wolf and he, that of the bear. When he shifted, she would not fear him. Bill could see in her eyes that she too shared his magic, weather she knew it or not. As a wolf, someday she would run by his side through the forests of their wild world.

Dinner was exceptional that evening. Cara and Bill ate their fill and savored every bite. Glowing in the light of the fire, they sat holding each other and began talking. The two told tales of their thrilling journeys, of their old village and of what they saw inside themselves and in each other.

After dining Risk was quick to Cara's side. Sitting pressed to her leg, he relaxing and waiting like a stone. The pack crowded in on the two humans and their fire. Their eyes shimmered like mirrors when flashed by the light of the flames. One by one, the wolves settled in to rest and digest around the fire. At first Rage had stayed in the shadows but was soon coaxed by Granite to join the group around the fire. Curled up in balls of wolf, Granite and Rage dozed off from the warmth of the fire while Risk sat alert beside his Cara. Aqua was stretched out at her feet, gazing up at Cara from time to time. They were still a bit unsure about Bill, for he was little more than a stranger to them.

The fire began to die down and a chill began to set in. The night had shifted in it's sleep, allowing the cold to creep through the star painted blanket that covered the land. There was a break in the dance of conversation. An intermission, a rest in speech. Looking into the night, Bill began to sing. It was then that Aqua chose to bounce over to him like a puppy desperately seeking an elder's attention.

The grey wolf put a paw on Bill's knee and slapped his tail on the ground rhythmically. Aqua was infatuated by Bill's songs. He had always loved to hear Cara sing but Bill sang new songs, and they made Cara giggle and smile. Aqua wasn't sure if her loved Cara's endless laughter of the bouncing of Bill's tune's more. Showing off for Bill,

Aqua saw Cara smile. It made Aqua pull back his black lips an join her in a silly grin.

He decided he liked Bill and even liked the horses. They were funny looking animals that smelled like straw and sage and butter. Aqua knew butter from Cara and the village, and these beasts reminded him of the fatty, rich butter he so loved. In fact, butter was one of the few things he could think of that he loved more than chasing horses. Butter and Bill's songs. Next to chasing horses, those were his favorite things.

"I think, I think he wants you to sing to him, Bill." Cara's words were chopped up by the giddy laughter that erupted as Aqua beat the grass like a drum. Risk twisted his head back at Cara. He was laughing at his baby brother's performance. Eyes flashing with a playful happiness, Risk asked Cara,

"Are you sure that's my brother? There is no way that pup shares my bloodline! Is there?? "

Laughter was the only response.

"Look Risk, he's even keepin' a beat for me!"

Cara just continued to laugh at Bill and her brothers. Then, Bill began to sing.

Buckets of snow, coming down on me.
Brings me no sorrows, I only feel glee.
My horses run slow, when they are cold.
Wolf Woman tells me my father grew mean, as he grew old.
I've found this wild creature; she's here now with me.
I hope to always be with her, wild and free.

The spirits, they come to me in dreams.
The show me the future, and all kinds of things.
We are to stay here, with me and my love, Cara just might
For soon a new purpose will unfold, waiting in the morning light.

Let me tell you what will come.
With the rising of a morning sun,
People from places, ages and time,
Will be here to work, but not for a dime.
A log castle will be given
For the people to work, play and live in.
They will study life, our creatures and our land.

We must revive the earth, and take a stand.
Teaching other countries, showing them the way
This will be the purpose of our everyday.
Cara will run this brand new place
And I will be here, letting no love go to waste.

Aqua licked Bill's face in thanks and approval but the song was
not what he had expected.
"Sorry buddy"
Bill said as he scratched behind Aqua's ears,
"It started out to be funny."
Bill sighed, and then shrugged off his embarrassment from his
short versed song.
"I just have to sing what I feel, and that came from outside of
me. A spirit song."
"Wow Bill. That... is *our* prophecy?"
Risk cut in,
"Seems to be. There was power in those play words. Even my
puppy of a brother can see that."
Aqua agreed, and gave a mock bark to Risk. Bill cleared his
throat,
"So these two are brothers, then?"
Cara's eyes went wide and Risk closed his mouth to swallow.
How could Bill know? Cara said nothing of the pack's relations yet,
they hadn't even been fully introduced. Was it possible that he too,
understood the wolves? Cara rubbed her eyes in attempt to clear her
thoughts.
"Yeah, I mean yes. Yes they are brothers, technically. I mean a
few years apart but same parents, ya know. How did you know that? I
don't think I've told you about all that yet, have I?"
"Sure haven't, but then again I haven't told you everything yet
either. Darlin' I speak to my horses. I speak with the birds. I'll even
have a conversation with a caribou, not that it'd be worth it, though."
"I just... didn't know you could understand them, I mean us,
too!"
It was as if they were high, it was impossible not laugh and
smile. Bill, Aqua, Cara and Risk giggled and smiled until a humbling
silence came across the valley. It was at this point when they realized
the fire had died and the night was almost gone. It was time to retreat
to the cabin for the remains of the evening.

Cara as Bill began to walk towards the cabin, the silver brothers trailing at their heels.

Aqua remembered then how much he had once enjoyed sleeping inside. It was like the den from his memories: warm, safe and close to family. Risk however, felt unsure of the sleeping arrangements. In a bed, Bill and Cara curled up side by side as he and her once did. Now he was on the floor, unable to feel Cara's soft warmth that he had grown so accustomed to. Aqua contently curled up by the foot of the bed while Risk stood up and paced.

All of a sudden, he stopped and stared. Bill was not his replacement. This was what made Cara the happiest and seeing her innocent face Risk saw that there was no betrayal here. She loved Bill and he loved her greater in return. She still loved Risk, and he loved her. Nothing there had changed.

Looking out the window, Risk saw the rest of his pack and was put at ease. He had a prophecy of his own, even if Bill was unable to sing it, it was clear. This would become his territory as much as it was Bill's and the horses. There was game, there was water, there was love. The third is never so easy to come by but always a virtue to a wolf. Once again, beside Cara Risk had found a new meaning to "home". Stretching long, nails tearing up thin curls of the soft wood floor, Risk prepared for a happy sleep on the cool floor at Cara's bed side.

**.

For the next month, the days went by with great speed. Every moment was packed with love, life and much joy. There was no drama or stress in their lives in the valley. Nothing but strength and happiness dwelled in their home. It all seemed to fall into place. After all the struggles and adventures, peace had settled upon them all. Plus, Cara was fully happy. She had found friends in the horses. There was one young steed in particular that she had grown quite fond of. His name was Dusty.

Dusty was a three year-old male, feisty and fast. He was a golden stallion with a coat that glistened as if it were infused with specks of gold and copper. His mane was the shade of raw sweet corn, light blond with a tinge of yellow. Before Dusty grew aware of Cara's friendship, he would spend his days racing through the fields and across the mountain ridge, whining with an untamed passion. He was unlike any of the other horses in the herd and though a few shared similar coloring, Dusty always stood out.

It was his thrill seeking attitude that won over Cara. Bill explained how he often struggled with Dusty, the rambunctious youngster. Dusty was manageable before he became a loner, at east, according to Bill. It was just recently that Dust's best friend, a stallion by the name of Thunder, had run off. Whispering Bill searched for days. Riding out with his mare Agility, they looked with every hour of the sun. Bill was afraid that Thunder, who was every bit as wild as his golden counterpart, was lost to the blowing wind. Sometime the wind just seems to push creatures away, and bring them to the next place they belong.

Back to the story. Within a few days of playful spying on Dusty, the stallion began to make himself available to Cara. It seemed that he was as enchanted with the wolf woman as she was with him and his golden hide. After cautious introductions, the two promptly became companions. It soon became that Cara spent large quantities of her days off riding with Dusty in the cold, crisp air. Often times the Sedalia pack followed, Risk usually running by Dusty's side.

The group outings worked out well. Dusty was in love with the stealth and power the wolves commanded. He was unaware of how the wolves envied his fragile grace. Running with the pack Dusty found that they were the few of many he had encountered that could keep up with him and indulge in his rough-housing games. Dusty would snort, charge and kick like a bull. That of course was when he wasn't taunting others with his speed and cunning.

And so it was that the pack accepted Dusty as one of their own. For in the herd, Dusty had few companions. He was viewed as a bit of a bully. The mares and foals shied away from him while the stallions viewed him mostly as competition or a threat. But now, he had the wolves ad he was glad.

Indeed it was Aqua who was most taken by the spirit horse. Larger, stronger, and smarter than the domestic steeds, Dusty was every inch of a fairy tale horse. Aqua had seen horses. The few that dwelled in the village often looked cold, hungry and dull. They were skittish animals who whinnied from so little as his predator scent on the breeze. Even as a mere wolfling! But Dusty was the opposite of all that. He challenged Aqua to races, climbs and snow angels. To Rage and Granite, there was nothing more amusing than watching the horse and wolf wiggle on their backs in the snow, stirring up clouds of sparkling powder in their wake.

****

Cara Sedalia and Whispering Bill filled their days riding horses, keeping fires, doing chores, and making love. The spirits smiled down at union of the two wild souls and blessed their days with good food, warmth, and happiness. Whispering Bill's prophecy had yet to come true, though visions of his words came to Cara in dreams. It was in the depth of the night, looking into his eyes and laying by his side that she saw the most beautifully profound images. It burned inside of her soul like a campfire, often crackling and stirring her soul to dance like the very flames that dwelled inside her. She knew something was coming, and the anticipation made her giddy. Cara occasionally rose from her sleep, only to race through the forest, blindly searching for answers. It did not make her unhappy; she just wanted to be prepared. It seemed to be that waiting was the hardest part.

The seasons grew from fall to winter, and snow fell on the humble cabin layer by layer. Outside, the wolves could often be spotted curled up under a bushy overhang or buried under piles of the white snow. For fun the pack watched the snow fall as if it was a sport, cheering when the wind kicked up a snow spiral and watching the form of every flake as it clung to the icy ground. Yet from the piles of fur Cara often saw the wolves piled up in, it seemed that blizzard watching was purely a spectator sport.

Aqua and Risk were the only members of the pack who spent time inside with the humans. Rage scoffed at the idea of a wolf indoors. Meanwhile, Granite seemed to have better things to do than sit beside a dancing fire, like showing of for Rage. Courting the red female had become his favorite past time. Out of all the wolves in the pack, it was Aqua who found himself in love with every bit of the bear man's lifestyle.

Aqua was thrilled to pull firewood home and haul loads aside the horses. After a long day's work, Aqua was rewarded with sings and a feast from Bill. It was picturesque how on the coldest nights, the bed inside the cabin was nothing but a heap of bodies and fur. Risk on the feet of his woman, and Aqua covering his man. And so it became that Aqua's role as a member of the Sedalia pack began to decrease as his time at Bill's side increased. Some things just came to be. The wolves were not upset by Aqua's straying nature, even if it was leaning towards a form of domestication. Risk even understood it, though he could never tame his spirit enough to settle as a pet. Though perhaps Aqua was more than that. More of a friendship than a form of domestication. Besides, life with Bill and Cara was good and could make any creature happy. Risk loved Cara and her human mate but he still felt the pull of the wild. He was a wolf, not a dog and inside he knew he had more to discover. His story could not simply end here.

The horses were strong and well fed throughout the winter; they pulled through it with great strength. Spring was beginning to approach and on days when the snowfall was mild, Bill would ride his favorite leading mare Agility out into the forest behind the cabin. Behind them the heard would follow the starch white mare and it's mount into the wilderness.

When Cara joined the ride, she rode the rebellious youth Dusty, time after time. Often the other horses got jealous of the copper youth speeding through the snow with such a radiant mount. After the long ride, when night fell, the herd's jealousy was replaced by admiration and awe. He who was previously the outcast and the fool became an icon and a hero to his breed. All for his speed and swift footwork.

To pass the time through the long storms, the couple would sit inside by the fire, drinking strong drinks and smoking dried summer herbs. It was then when the spirits spoke the most, and told Cara to be ready for the White Tiger in late spring. After finally getting an answer to satisfy her undying curiosity, her mind was put at a bit of an ease and Cara instantly felt her body relax. In the moments to follow, she felt a strange tingling change come over her. She wanted to leap from cloud to cloud, to kiss the stars, to drink the sun, it felt so good. she had to run, and she wanted to tell the pack.

Leaving Bill inside and intoxicated, Cara ran out into the snow. Dressed only in Bill's flannel shirt and home-made moccasins, she plunged into the knee-deep snow, climbing like a cougar over ice packs to find her wolves. Though the weather was harsh, the frigid wind did not chill her. She laughed and the fire roared inside her, keeping her warm. She was fully alive. Even her eyes were newly awake, picking up every detail in the meadow. Her senses screamed for she felt is if she could hear every little flake of snow tearing through the air and hitting the ground. Her nose wiggled, and she smelled the fresh, clean scent of snow wetting the forest off in the distance. Though her sense soared, Cara saw nothing of the wolves. Focusing she howled softly, trying not to disturb the horses. There was nothing. Perhaps they were out hunting. Her thoughts were blinking like a strobe light and she could no longer hold her attention on the wolves. Her body convulsed, maybe from the cold, maybe from the ecstasy. Either way, her body flailed to the ground and her mind began to slip away.

"What is this?"

Her speech was slurred, even in thoughts to herself.

A soothing darkness engulfed her vision, covering the word she was looking at until all she saw; even with eyes wide open was black. Time seemed to stop. She grew blind, deaf numb and was unable to breathe.

All of a sudden, Cara convulsed violently, and everything came back. Feeling surged through her body, as if she could feel every atom of every molecule in her composition buzzing and toughing and making her exist. There came a pain that started pulsing through her fingers. The inner walls of her stomach began to itch and move, causing her to arch her back in a stretch. Everything was moving, everything was alive. A powerful gust of wind picked up and threw ice daggers at her thighs. Cara gasped in shock and bared her teeth at the arctic gusts challenging her. She propelled of the ground, landing on her feet and biting at the wind. A wave of conscience passed through her and she stopped. What was she doing?

The wind stopped but it wasn't over. Cara dropped to the snow and stretched her body in an S in attempt to relieve the sensations pulsing through her torso. She clawed at the ice beneath her, trying to ease the pain of her fingers. It did not help. The tingling pulling feeling became greater and further spread through her body. Fingers now burning like those hot with frostbite, Cara balled her hands up into fists and stretched her legs as they too, began to itch and pull. Cara drank in the frozen air and exhaled a snarl made of her own hot breath. Again, she drank. This one opened her mouth so that her jaw might pop back into place and at least that part would cease. But it didn't.

She was loosing her vision and could only see in spiraling waves that made her dizzy when she opened her eyes. Wanting to throw up, Cara lie in the snow, stretching and snarling and feeling things a human would never know were possible to feel. Her hips were being pulled apart inside her, her shoulder blades slid against her rib cage, her spine was being realigned and her organs slurped and sloshed inside her body to compensate for her mutation. It was then that her heart slowed down to the beat of time and it seemed an eternity went by in total agony.

Time continued to warp around Cara as she lay in twitching torment, frozen in snow and time. She hadn't been gone long when Whispering Bill finally came out to find her. It was not unusual for Cara to dart off into the woods without telling him. Something about the gleam in her eye when Cara darted off made him believe that something was happening. Breathing out the last puff of smoke from his pipe, Whispering Bill stepped outside. Looking around, he did not see Cara, nor could he find the pack. The snow was cycloning in a flurry when all of a sudden, it stopped and the air grew still. Diamond flakes twinkled their way down until the melted into the snow. Blinking into the night Bill looked again, this time with better clarity.

Out in the valley, not more than twenty feet from his door, Whispering Bill saw a hint of movement. It was then that he got trapped in the stare of a pale silver wolf. It was looking at him through strangely familiar golden eyes.

Twelve
~~~~~~~~~~~~~~~~~~~~~~~~~

Cara's eyes shot up when she heard the screen door of the cabin slam. The wind had stopped and everything was still. It was like an entirely different planet, everything looked and seemed... strange. Looking around Cara saw things she had never noticed before, and smelled scents buried beneath the frozen tundra. It was as if all her senses had been violently magnified. Everything everywhere was completely and thoroughly alive, saturated in motion.

She took four steps forward and listened to every crystal of ice crack and cry beneath her. Her nose twitched and swung her head to the right. Coming from the cabin was a voice. She was unable to make out who was staring at her, or what it was saying. The wind and snow kicked up again, apparently giving the speaker a curtain to hide their figure.

Bill watched the wolf from the cabin. His eyes followed it as she hesitantly stepped back towards the woods. Bill called to it,

"Brother, Sister, wolf! Do not be afraid, we here offer you no harm. But I do ask, where do you come from?"

When the canine did not respond, Bill took a deliberate step towards the wolf, testing to see if it would dart off into the woods. Though the beast was clearly alert and cautious, it did not appear to be afraid. Feeling the wind slice and tear at his naked flesh, Bill shivered as he stuffed his hands inside the pockets of his bull hide pants. Squinting through the blowing ice, Bill began to close the distance between him and the wolf. He wanted to hear its thoughts and touch it's luxurious silver fur.

Cara felt her hip muscle twitch as she waited for the body of the talking voice to appear. It was hard to see him amidst the spastic snow flurries. Thus, in being approached by the unknown, her new body told her to run. Perhaps her brain lost it's sense in the snow, for instead of darting off as she should, she scolded her wolf and remained where she stood. Was it curiosity that killed the wolf as well?

Heavy steps creaked across the ice-crusted meadow and grew louder as they came closer. Side stepping in a complete circle, Cara turned her body so that she may greet this visitor head on, face to face. With her senses straining against the cold and her body tensed and ready to move, she thought she was prepared for meeting when an ice crystal managed to sting her on the nose and cause her to blink and sneeze. When she looked up, the wind held a suspenseful pause and the powder settled into the snow.

The weather was playing tricks on her again. Her brother didn't know when to stop.

A great grizzly bear sat before a silver wolf. Cara did not run as those of her kind should. From this fellow predator, she felt no threat. It was the figure that matched the voice and he was close enough that she could smell the scents of his breath and fur, and the musk from his glands. His coat fit him like a tailored gentleman's jacket. It hugged every massive muscle of the bears body and yet hung off the flesh with such custom perfection, giving him well defined mass and size. The fur was ever-changing in its color appearance. His hairs were flecked with all shades of gold, red, brown, white and black. It gave him the appearance of having a prismatic coat.

The eyes of the bear were the endless spectrum of colors that graced the valley in summer, and that was familiar. Cocking her head to the side, Cara breathed in the presence of her visitor. He was the human voice, in a bear's body. In return to the wolf's advances and inspections, the bear curled his lips to better conduct his study of her.

The next morning, Bill and Cara woke up side by side in the living room floor. The shifting was over. What they were left with seemed like little more than a dream. Last night they revealed their inner beasts to each other and went out running wildly through the woods. Side by side they sang to the moon as they raced across the evergreen wilds, seeing nothing but passing trees and each other. Feeling supremely alive, knowing more than one can think to ponder and seeing the world in constant motion all around them was bliss. That memory would forever make an impression.

Last night, owls watched as a wolf cried at the side of a roaring Kodiak bear. Last night, an arctic fox was the victim of a bear's game of chase. Last night, teeth clattered and blood was sported as a wolf and a grizzly wrestled each other in violent affection. Cara and Bill had bonded on a new level. Now, their spirits were linked with their bodies, human and beast alike.

****

Winter passed by like a stone rolling down a mountain, with spring arriving with the same sudden impact of a speeding stone. Patches of snow were shrinking and the warming temperatures loosened Cara's body and made her shifting more intense. The shifting was no new ability. The only new aspect was that finally, Cara had recognized her power or what it was. Pain often comes from realization, no matter how grand the given gift may be. Struggling for survival en route to the Harvest Valley had distracted her from the transformations. They just simply *were*. The wolves however, all viewed Cara as neither wolf nor human. Rather as a creature of all her own. Not that they didn't accept her, for she led them like the alpha she was. It was just the overall nature of the beast that allowed her to stand alone.

For most creatures in the valley, spring was a time of lush enjoyment. With the warming of the earth came new life, new food and well deserved relaxation. For Cara, it was a time of dedicated spiritual preparation. She was being visited nightly in dreams by great spirits such as the wise owl, the noble buffalo and the greatest of all, the white tiger. Her time of duty was drawing near. A persistent vision revealed to her that soon, very soon, small flocks of people from around the world were on their way to the valley, via the spirit breeze, to aid her in her divine purpose in restoring the balance. Cara was the divine individual designed by the spirit's themselves, to bridge the barrier of man and nature. Through protection, exploration and modern devices; such as books, videos and TV shows, Cara and her crew would someday, educate humans and animals enough to understand each other and bring back the balance between beast and man.

While her destiny was well defined, the new spring brought new smells, new life and new ideas to Cara. On one particular night, in the youth of it's darkness, Cara was laying in the cozy bed she shared with Bill. It was soft and strong, made up of layers of hides and down. Beside her mate snored quietly, motionless as he dreamt of her. She yawned anxiously, wishing his peaceful sleep could consume her as well. For hours now, Cara had fought off sleep, much to her remorse. Even as she watched her bear-man's chest rise and fall, she was restlessly wide awake.

With Bill asleep, Cara felt completely alone inside the cabin. The entire pack had been out every night lately, celebrating the new seasons and singing to the stars. It was on this lonely night that she also felt deserted by the pack. The more she thought about hr feelings, the more she struggled to define it. It seemed the massive consuming emotion was made up of a combination of feelings; Hurt, sadness, confusion and eager anxiety that triggered her restlessness. She had nothing else to do tonight and so closing her eyes, Cara further dissected her current state of mind.

Firstly, she was hurt that she was invited to be out running with the pack. They were bonding closer as wolves while she bonded with her man. It wasn't bad; it was only that tonight the wolves were outside running while she was indoors, attempting routine sleep even though she was anything but tired. It was spring and the horses had a schedule she helped maintain. Besides, Bill had had a long day and his body required the sleep that hers so rudely rejected and to sleep peacefully, he needed her by his side. Whispering Bill was a strong man but time had revealed that his strength was dependant on Cara's constant love and comfort. The discovery was the reason she had not left him to run with the wolves tonight. Also, even though it was difficult, maybe this change was good. She had to prepare for a new role, and the pack no longer needed her as once, they had. To Risk she had given much of her knowledge and wisdom and he would use it to help in the battle of preservation and understanding.

Trailing into her next thought, Cara was confused. Why was she so torn? She knew that she was not a wolf the same way the members of her pack were and that they had their own lives to live. They needed to grow strong as a wolf pack to teach the other wolves of their proper roles in nature. To keep the canines strong, and protect them from danger. The life of a new pack would arise. New blood, hopefully even spirit blood. Risk's pack. The idea warmed her. He had become an alpha, strong and reliable, it was clear. Despite morale conflict of living with another alpha, he dare not challenge Cara for dominance. Either way pack dynamics were getting harder, especially around the other wolves where Risk had to define his rank and position.

Knowing the strengths and limitations of her wolf form, she could easily beat Risk down and run the pack, but then he would desire a mate and would never be able to find another like the grizzly, Bill. So living her life as a sterile alpha female would be impossible, and the option of running as a lone wolf was clearly out of the question. As was leaving the pack entirely. Cara imagined her feelings of not wanting to let go were similar for mothers and fathers alike. No matter what, she knew there would always be a longing to lead the pack. In addition it would forever conflict the details of her destiny and alter the result of her fate. But where did she need to be? The answers always came through riddles. Really, in the end, who determines the need? She knew the world's problems. What about her? It didn't matter. She couldn't even make up her own mind on where she wanted to be. Here with her mate waiting to be the profit of the Tiger, or out on four legs, free and simple with the pack? If she left now, could she even find the pack? Cara blinked back a tear; she didn't need to interfere with them tonight. That's where the sadness came in.

Pack dynamics were changing. Away from Cara, Risk became able to devout more time to better leading, hunting and survival techniques. Something's just come with wild instinct but something's could only be learned from experience and time.

So Cara watched the Sedalia pack's dynamics. Her place and rank never shifted even though they had not been out on a pack hunt but once together sense life in the Harvest valley began. Also, Risk had become sexually mature, and every pack member knew it. His urine reeked of hungry male. By fall, Risk would take a mate and the legacy of the Spirit Wolf would continue. Cara had no right to interfere with that course of fate. Inside it's what she wants for Risk, Granite, Rage and perhaps even Aqua. Even though he seemed more content at the cabin and would doubtfully last long with the pack. He would never be traded like a common dog though she would still feed him and could still use his help. Having the blue eyed canine would be like keeping a treasure from the years past's adventures. So the idea of the pack leaving, though it was right and necessary, made her sad.

Cara's restless eagerness was the strongest underlying emotion. Her life felt stagnant and she couldn't take it anymore. Something needed to happen.

Now.

****
***

Getting out of bed, Cara's feet snapped and popped as they touched the cold wooden floor. The sleeping bear did not wake. Without grabbing a coat or shoes, Cara walked quietly outside to the front porch. Closing the door quietly, a shining shape in the sky caught her attention. It was the moon, cut straight down the middle.

"Perfect"

She said in a whisper, it mirrored just how she felt. Taking two steps and ending in a pivot, Cara turned her body so it faced the moon and the icy glow shone blue on her skin. Closing her eyes she took a deep breath and her body shivered violently. It was cold. Too cold for naked skin. She needed fur.

Opening her eyes slowly, like a child waking from a dream, she took another deep breath.

Inside, her body had been itching all night. Even while she lay in bed with Bill, her bones itched. Despite their attempts, the fresh air and deep breaths did not soothe her. Still she was awake, restless and itchy. Grinning a wide, sly smile, Cara spoke aloud once more,

"Guess I'm not sleeping tonight."

With that, she jumped down the stairs and hit the ground running. Across the flat plane of the valley she ran until her heart hammered in her ears allowing her to lunge forward and let go of her body. It began to control itself as the human mind slipped away. Her arms gladly extended to meet the earth for the next bound. Instead of hands hitting frosted grass, black wolf pads touched the ground, surrounded by grey fur. Her human hips and spine quickly relocated, in cooperation. Joints and sockets realigned with the sound of tree branches snapping in two. A finale human exhale before her organs squished and expanded, then her hind legs hit the ground. Cara's silver tail bobbed behind her as her wolf form shot through the frill to the hills and mountains. When running, wolves never look back.

Thirteen
~~~~~~~~~~~~~~~~~~~~~~~~~~~~~~~~~~~~~

   The frost-coated wolf slowed her pace once she cleared the foothills and began her trek up the mountain. When crossing the hills, she had not seen nor caught scent of any other wolf. But the wind had been fierce and patches of snow and ice were few and scattered across the terrain. It was hard to track them. Perhaps still, they were close by. Human logic fading away, her last refined thought was of the pack, and her acceptance. With her being gone from their lives so often, did it even matter if she came to them? And if she found them, would she even want to see them? The whole human/wolf boundaries had recently become all the more real, living with Whispering Bill. But then again there were times that he too, was no longer human. What an overload. With a snort of disgust, the wolf logic clicked on; her irrationalizes and endless questions clicked off.
   It felt so good to be out, the pushing feeling of "I need to go some where or do something" had mostly faded away. The familiar scent of her own wolf musk wrapped around her and made her feel warmer and stronger. She picked her pace back up and let out her favorite howl, calling to all things and spirits. It was her telling the infinite worlds that she was awake, alive and above all, she was here. Silence echoed her call, although it was a different silence then most, it was as if the trees and creatures were listening for more from the kindred caller. It didn't matter; the wolf wasn't waiting for a response. They knew she was here. The silver wolf was out now and with her nose to the ground, she planned on finding what it was that her body itched for.
   Climbing cliffs, mauling mountains and winding through forests, Cara ran for what seemed like an endless eternity. The

mountains had become her rivals and she felt the need to climb them
and master them all. She mastered her challenge, though it took her
through the life of the night. At the end of her sport, the she-wolf
stood in the mist, lost in the clouds, panting atop the tallest mountain
looking over the Harvest Valley and beyond. The sun was beginning
to rise far off in the east and Cara was glad to have a place to stop and
catch her breath.

Eyes narrowing like those of a hawk, she studied the landscape
in search of the simplest of things. Movement. A sign of food, life,
friend or foe. Nostrils flaring, the wolf attempted to catch a scent, she
was fully alert. She found nothing and was put at ease. *Safety*. Sitting
lazily on her haunches her ears twitched and turned to double check
for any foreign sounds. All the wolf could hear was the blowing of the
wind, the rustle of remaining trees and shrubs and the flowing of a
river, all off to the east. The Harvest Valley was to the west, and her
mountain was in the middle.

Sensing no danger, Cara curled up in the familiar ball of fur she
was so used to seeing. A wolfy smile still curled her lips when she
indulged in this common pose. All her life she had watched the wolves
and dogs sleep in this position of ultimate comfort and protection. At
last she was able to do what had always been a fantasy. It was
everything she had always thought it to be.

The she-wolf awoke a few hours later, casually as a hound on a
sunny patio. She stretched her legs that, as she stretched, she realized
they were kicked up in the air. Opening her eyes she looked around
slowly to study her surroundings. Still lazily relaxed, Cara's autumn
eyes observed the mid morning sky. It was clear of clouds and seemed
to be sparkling from the sun's unblocked rays. It was because of the
cloudless morning that Cara found herself in this position. Sprawled
on her back, tummy exposed to the warmth of the yellow day star.

Rolling on her side, her back was turned to the valley, and her
focus remained on the sun. Closing her eyes, she stretched once more.
This time she was listening to her mussels expand, her bones pop and
her heart beat come alive from sleep. With a final yawn, the wolf was
awake. Letting out a huff of air, she stood and once more, surveyed
her surroundings.

The sweet-yet-bitter scent of juniper berries tickled her nose on
the breeze. One triangular ear twitched and, pointing her muzzle to
the right, she listened for strange sounds in her environment.
Nothing. While she could have been dreaming, she thought she had

heard a consistent, though distant, small sound in the distance It had sounded like voices, human voices. The silver wolf huffed in frustration.

The possibility of humans outside the valley was mystifying and unheard of. What was she thinking? Besides, where there voices sounded from seemed like an unlikely place for a human dwelling. Past a few rocky slopes a rigid rock structure opened up into a canyon, the view from here did not show it as an area able of supporting life. Cara would have to get closer to understand better. She wanted to explore. Her wolf brain scolded her idea of searching for humans though if she needed logic to explain her human spontaneity to her wolf, she was out of luck. Just in time her stomach rumbled, and now that she was hungry hr wolf has happy to run off.

After dining on an unsuspecting ground squirrel, Cara headed off in search of the voices to the east. The terrain was deadly. After traveling across the mountain for as far as her four paws could carry her, Cara faced the jagged cliffs of the canyon. The landscape would be difficult to cover for either wolf or woman, but it was beautiful and a rare sight for such a climate. The bare rock acted like a shell, protecting the layers of life that thrived inside the canyon. It was like a life vacuum; while the outer layers of cliff and stone remained rocky and barren, in the depths of the canyon trees grew and green leafy plants were booming. A river wound between the cliffs, leading to a gushing waterfall at the end of the gorge. The scent of the crisp water reminded the wolf how thirsty she had let herself become. The sound of the raging water alerted the woman inside to how dangerous getting a drink could be.

****

It was the birth of the afternoon as the sun hung in the middle of the cloudless blue sky. The wolf was panting hard, limbs shaking as she clung to the walls of the canyon. A herd of dall sheep seemed to mock her from across the gorge. They leapt effortlessly from cliff to cliff, never once loosing their footing, acridly even budging a pebble. The silver wolf stopped to snarl and bark at them, after half an hour they were becoming a distraction. The members of the herd flinched, with eyes growing big and panicked at the wolf's threat. Some even bolted out of sight. Their fear gave Cara enough satisfaction to return to the struggle of climbing along the canyon walls.

Rocks crumbled beneath her, falling down into a silent grave until at last they hit the bottom and made a loud thud from the impact. Crunch, clatter clatter, bang and crash. The rocks fell beneath her and her claws dug into rock with every step. *Is that what I would sound like if I were to slip?* She wondered.

Finally Cara came to a crevice where she could stop to catch her breath and gather her strength once more. The morning snack no longer satisfied her and urgent hunger toyed with her wolf mind, stealing her focus from the climb. The wolf would not lie down So instead she sat and began looking both ways to survey her progress. It seemed her adventure had brought her to the middle of the canyon. There was no way up and out of the gorge and the way down was less than desirable. Even the way back looked painfully difficult, at best, while the way forward made her tuck her tail beneath her. *Am I stuck?* Cara let out a frustrated wolfy huff. A wolf was not designed to be a cliff climber, she knew that. The dall sheep had seemed out of sight sense their last confrontation until now it seemed. A young ram yawned lazily, and the herd stared at her once more. They were having no difficulty traveling along the gorge. Maybe there was power in being a sheep, Cara thought to herself. Then she thought about what easy prey they would make once she arrived on flat land, and she doubted it.

Leaving bloody paw prints behind, the wolf returned to the climb. Above, the sun was growing hot on the slick of her back and her left side. Her right side brushed against the rock, noticeably cold in comparison. After landing another difficult jump, Cara began to hear the murmur of voices once again. This time, they were real, and, they were close. There seemed to be a great many of both men and women. Triangular ears swiveling, she did not hear any high pitched tones that would indicate children. Often times their voices and laughter reminded Cara of birds. The people were not moving towards her and she was down wind, they presented no current threat to the wolf other than being human in the first place. For that, the wolf inside her was thankful. It still resisted to Cara's command of investigation, but she knew her spirit would overcome the body of the beast.

It was one of the last jumps before reaching the plateau with the waterfall and, sure enough, it would prove to be the most difficult. The gap between the cliff she stood on now and that which she aimed to land upon did not seem to far. The drop below her however, plunged down hundreds of feet deep into the belly of the gorge. It would be an easy death.

Stepping back from the edge, the silver wolf shook her coat free of dust and rock. Stretching out her broken claws as much as possible, she used them as cleats to keep her footing as she ran. One-two-three-four, one-two-three-four, one-two-three-four, one-two- and the wolf was launched into the air.

Three-four and she landed. Then she slipped. Hind paws clawing and kicking in the wind she panicked and clawed at the rocks until she found a thorny shrub to claw into. Her legs and forepaws bled profusely as she used the thorn brush to pull her weight back up the slope. The panic of death rang in her mid like a shrill, loud alarm. Her belly shimmied over the shrubs jutting out of the rock as her legs continued franticly clawing and kicking away from the empty air. Her claws shaved the stone and a few even broke off. Burrs caught her sides and thorns whipped her face until her paws finally felt the top of the cliff. Giving a final kick to the wind, Cara thrust her hind legs onto the ledge. With solid ground beneath her paws the wolf was able to stand long enough to watch as rocks trickled down the rock she stood on. In seconds they shook loose large boulders causing a loud commotion. It seemed merely white noise now.

Struggling and breathing hard Cara hurried to climb to the peak of the isolated plane she was on; from there she could jump to the flat top of the plateau that lead to the waterfall. Her belly rumbled and she sighed. She hoped the waterfall would also provide an easy meal and a place to lick hr wounds. Once at the peak of the isolated rock, she found herself in great pain and exhausted. Panic signals once more sounded off inside of her. If she did not jump soon, she would collapse and be hounded by buzzards and torn apart by the wind, if not pushed into the canyon. One last bound.

Gathering the remains of her strength and adrenaline, she ignored the patched of blood and her red, broken claws beneath her. Haunches bunching up, she leapt into the air and on landing; she lost her footing once more.

Falling down the knife shaped rocks, her spine twisted, her legs were thrown from beneath her and fur was ripped away in ribbons. Her howl of terror turned into a scream of the same as her tumbling body shifted into a bloody human form. The beast was to scared, and to stressed to remain in its form. Cara could not see what was happening, she didn't even feel pain as her limp form rolled over thorns, stones and jagged slices of ice. The winter had difficulty letting go of this piece of rack and the cold wind came, only to rip away Cara's last attempts to grab something to hold onto. Her body became lead. A lethal blow into a tree trunk knocked her out while also suspending her fall. Her arm hung awkwardly in the air, reaching for the pit of the canyon below.

In the black room that Cara knew as her unconscious state, all was quiet at last. Even the wicked screeching of the wind had vanished. It was odd though, how it had gone from a warm sunny day to one of measurable chill and vicious ice and winds. After floating for some time in her black room, Cara heard frantic footsteps coming her way. They were light, swift footsteps moving quickly towards her black room. One-two-one-two, the rhythm of a human. The steps were two light to be Bill, perhaps a small boy. But she heard no children in the voices, it must be another woman.

The gravel crunched a few feet away from Cara's body; did the light-stepping woman see her? It hurt, but another wave of panic forced her to open her blood shot eyes and attempt to view the imposer. Through one eye, all Cara could see was red. Through the other, all she saw was the walls of the canyon and on the bottom, a line of blue sky. She was upside down and, craning her neck to locate herself, she realized there was nothing beneath her to support her from the shoulders up. She was bent in the middle, her top half dangling into the open mouth of the canyon. Her legs were somehow uncomfortably wrapped around the trunk of a tree. Cara closed her eyes instantly. She rejected the pounding pain that was all too eager to rush through her body.

As Cara got swallowed back into her little black room, the visitor began shouting and making all kinds of noise. Cara had to focus really hard to understand what she was saying.

"Oh god! Don't move! I'm here to help!"

It was the voice of the soft footed woman, Cara began to call her. It was ironic, for her voice even sounded like that of a young boy's. Her tone was too stern to tell the between the two, but Cara could sense the difference. The gentle touch on her ankle comforted her and confirmed the gender questioning; it was undoubtedly the soft hand of a woman. The softness seemed to fade as her grip tightened on Cara's ankles, as the woman began to pull Cara out of the air and onto the ground. The soft-footed woman swore under her breath, and then resumed speaking to Cara. Clearly, she was trying to keep the wolf woman conscious.

"Damnit woman, your heavier than you look." She let out a grunt from the struggle before continuing.

"Then again, you look like a mess. All this could be dead weight, making you twice as heavy."

She was talking in a guttural, growly voice for as she spoke she pulled Cara's body further from the edge and up a hill. This woman's ability to explain her own logic while saving a life made Cara giggle inside. Though still, her eyes were shut and she could only listen in the black room. She was like a child listening in on her parent's conversations when it was much past bed time. Cara recalled a distant memory. She couldn't see anything that was going on. She was forced to listen, unable to react to the words on the other side of the door. This experience was much like that one so many, many years ago.

"Come on girl, stay with me! Ugh....there we are, now you can't roll down that hill like it looks like you did before. Ok, now lets check your pulse."

The woman went silent; did she still have a pulse? Cara was curious what the woman would find.

"Oh my god, good. You're still alive! Wake up. Please, talk to me. Come on woman, you can look at me."

The woman was tapping Cara's cheek and forehead, the one thing that really irritated her. After a moments pass, the woman's tapping bothered Cara enough to groan and mumble an annoyed sound at the tapper.

"I hate people touching my face, I figured that might of worked! Thank the White Tiger you're alive. Although how, I'm not sure." Did she really just mention the White Tiger? And was that laughter Cara heard? Was her life saver laughing at her? She had to see this. Oh please, please, let her see this.

If anvils could be strapped on eyelids, they felt like they were on Cara's as she attempted to view the world. It was slow, but the curtains opened and the bright sun shrank her bowl sized pupils in an instant. Her head was in the woman's lap.

Cara was able to look up and she the sharply carved features of the smiling face above her. A hooked nose, a sharp jaw line and skinny, pointed lips curved in a warm smile. Her coloring was different from most faces Cara had seen in this life, and seeing light hair on tanned skin made her return the woman's smile. Her face was freckled like only one other she had seen in the village, and her eyes shone violet blue like Cara's favorite sage flower. Her savior was not from around here it seemed. She was not like anything Cara had ever seen, yet she looked vaguely familiar to her, like from another life, or another dream.

"My name is Beth. I can't believe I found you, I'm not supposed to stray away from the group but.... well I'm sorry. Anyway, can you speak? Who are you?" There was a pause and the breeze picked up enough to blow blond tresses of hair across Beth's face. Cara tried to speak but the words failed her, only a low growl came out.

"Grrrr....." was the only gargle of a noise Cara could make in response. She blinked and when she did, only one eyelid opened again. The blood had exploded in her right eye and her eyelid shaded it from further damage. A red tear did however, manage to escape. Beth wiped it off delicately with a skinny finger.

"Oh sweet spring, we need to take care of you but I can't leave you here to go find help. Uhf.....I can hear the group, they can't be far away but the sun is going to set soon and... and......." she was cut off because her patient, who seemed barely on the brink of survival, made efforts to move. Cara twitched at best. She did the only thing she could think of to save herself and her rescuer. She howled. It was crackly, and sounded more like a growl but Beth got the point. She hushed Cara and began calling out names and making enough noise to startle the ptarmigan out of the brush nearby.

It was then that Beth realized the shivers coming from the mountain woman. She had no cloths on, but the caking blood had made it seem otherwise. Unzipping her fleece wind breaker with much force and speed, Beth quickly covered Cara the best she knew how. The warm sunlight eliminated the painful possibilities of frost bite and other cold related ailments. So that and that alone allowed Beth to take in an easier breath as she waited for their rescue.

When Cara woke up, she found herself clean and dry. Her legs felt like led weights as she tried to move them. It was painful, but it could be done. Sitting up right, she finally opened her eyes and peered down at the scenery below. It was sunset, her favorite time of the day. Already she sensed herself trying to smile. She was at a camp; it was warm and smelled of roasting fat and wood smoke. She had been curled up under a heavy bear blanket, inside a tent that had been set up for the night. The flap was pulled open and so Cara looked through sleepy eyes at the pink sunlight that was cast upon the faces of her rescuers. It could have been delirium, or perhaps it was just a dream, but it was a very beautiful moment.

Fourteen
~~~~~~~~~~~~~~~~~~~~~~~~~~~~~~~~~~~~

Back at the cabin, Whispering Bill woke up alone. This was not the first time for him, he never knew what to expect, living with Cara. At first he always feared he would frighten her away, it was not easy living with a grizzly man. All to soon he discovered it was also quite an adventure living with a wild woman. It was Cara's free spirit that had made him fall in love with her, falling so hard that if her were to ever hit bottom, he would break into a thousand tear-shaped pieces. Life with her was exciting, and when he was with her he was always happy. It was when she went away that sorrow and loneliness dared to creep into his psyche. Though he knew she chased the wind, he made sure was never far behind.

Sitting alone on the wooden porch swing, Bill watched the steam rise from the earth. It circled around the trees and wrapped around the legs of his horses in the pasture. It was still very early, with the sun barely peaking over the mountains to the east. The rays that shone on his face felt warmer than usual. Following the rising sun up into the blue ocean of cloudless sky, he imagined where his mate might be. Probably off in the forest, sleeping. Or perhaps she was out with her pack, or had they returned? He called for Aqua who had become his closest friend and frequent companion from the pack. Two short whistles and a long last note, that the tune for his friend. He waited until a leaping figure emerged from the back of the house.

Aqua's face was wet with water and his jowls were streaked with blood. Coming to Bill with a wagging tail and perky ears he was content and alert, eager to assist. Bill couldn't help but let out a husky laugh. His voice was still groggy from sleep, making his tone deep and throaty if he were to speak. Aqua had been fishing in the lake behind his home, and from the smell and blood, it seemed he must have been successful.

"So is has the pack returned from the run?" Bill asked Aqua while rubbing the sides of the wolf's body. He was well fed but his coat was thinning for the spring and it made him look thin and scraggly.

"Everyone is resting down by the lake. We are all well fed and sleepy and I am become a skilled fish catcher!" Aqua's mouth was open and his pink tongue licked the sides of his muzzle to clean the remaining blood. There was a sparkle in his eyes, clearly seeking approval from Bill. He smiled and ruffled the slick fur that was Aqua's collar. One day the wolves would leave, Bill knew. But Aqua, it seemed was here to stay forever.

"Blue eyes, is Cara with you?" Addressing the blue-eyed wolf with this term was a form of endearment, for it was the name Cara called him by. Being aloud to use it was a blatant sign of their bond and Bill knew that their bond was a privilege.

"No bear-man, she is not. What's become of her this time?" Aqua sneezed out a laugh. It was funny to see Bill worry so over Cara. She always came back but there were times where he could see the human hurt, for he did not completely understand. He longed to be by her side every moment of the day

"Cara will settle down one day Bill." Aqua closed his mouth and ended his smile. Bill held Aqua's muzzle to his nose and laughed and said aloud,

"Gosh I hope not!" and together the two laughed and began to wrestle. If she were not back by dusk, he would go for a ride and if he was lucky, get to cross her path and bring her home with him.

After hardy play with the wolf, Whispering Bill tended to his horses and went inside to eat some stew. After filling up with Cara's cooking, he returned to his porch swing and smoked his pipe filled with grass fire. The birds sang a lullaby to him and he stretched out on the deck for a sun-soaked nap.

Bill began to dream and he dreamed of Cara in her wolf shape, a silver streak burning images into his mind. He saw her chasing skinny rabbits, wading through frigid rivers, racing in-between trees, rolling on her back in their fields and drinking the cool water from the lake. Lapping up the water with her delicate pink tongue, she looked up at him with those same hazel eyes he got lost in each night in bed. The colors of her eyes rippled like the pool of water she was drinking from. Glistening specks of gold flowed through streams of green the color of pine. The sepia-brown ring that circled her pupil dissolved and let the gold touch the black orb of pupil. It was magnificent.

Hours later, the coolness of the air made Whispering Bill rise. He had slept away the entire day and now, darkness flooded the valley. Pushing himself up he inhaled a deep breath to resurrect his heart rate. His skin prickled slightly from the cold as he slipped on his moccasins and headed off to the stables. The horses had put themselves away though some were still lazily munching on grass outside the barn. Agility, his trusted mare, came galloping towards him in a display of remarkable beauty. Her solid white coat reflected the coming moonlight and her mane seemed to make prisms with the fading lights. Through deep brown eyes, the color of Cara's rings in her own eyes, his second most treasured female locked eyes with him as she approached.

Sliding his hand up and down her face, Bill spoke gently to Agility and whispered sweet hellos. He had been by this mare's side at birth and would stay with her until death. She was a gift from his mother long, log ago. His very own spirit horse. She had turned out every bit as loyal and strong as he had ever hoped her to be. It was with her that he planned to ride tonight. Off into the moonlight, up into the hills tonight, he would let her lead them into the wilds.

****

Curled up at the foreign camp, Cara had still not left the safety of the tent, even as night fell. The faces of the people were strange to her, yet somehow they had a lingering trace of familiarity. A tall, dark man noticed Cara was awake and pondering. She noticed him watching her and managed to crack a smile. He returned her gesture, and waved a friendly hello as well. Breaking eye contact, the man turned his back to her and headed towards a glowing fire in the middle of the camp. Cara kept watching as the faces of men and women alike made a canvas for the dancing flame to play on. The fire light made everything seem warm and safe, and for the second time Cara was captured by the rural beauty of the place, the situation, and the people.

The dark man had tapped a light haired girl on the shoulder and pulled her out of the circle. Together, they looked Cara's way. It wasn't until the woman drew closer that Cara could recognize her. Walking on skinny stilt legs, carrying a bowl of food Cara realized it was Beth. The woman who walked on air. Her steps were so light, so effortless that Cara could hardly hear her walking. It was then that Cara saw the animal inside the woman, and it made her laugh though it hurt her ribs in doing so. Beth's light footing and delicate strength was that of a doe. Agile and alert, courageous and caring, Beth arrived by Cara's side. She knew that tonight the two of them would have some talking to do.

"Are you hungry?" Beth presented the bowl and it's continents. It was a rich, meaty stew and the smell made Cara's stomach growl with enthusiasm. She took the bowl. She was very hungry.

"Thank you." Was all Cara could say for as she sat up, she found that she had not been clothed. Setting the bowl down momentarily, she pulled the fur around her so that it covered her breasts and her lower body. It wasn't her nudity she covered for, with all her cuts and burses, Cara did not want to offend her hostess. Looking up at her, she thought she saw in her eyes the very offense that she had hoped to avoid. But that changed as soon as she picked the bowl up. Beth removed her scowl; she thought Cara rejected her food.

"Oh, I see. You have nothing to cover or be ashamed of. I thought you didn't like our food. It's my favorite stew and I helped make it."

Cara smiled her thanks, and then the two women just sat there. Cara was eating ravenously and Beth, as polite as she had been brought up to be, couldn't hide her amusement as she watched. All the time, an intensive study was being conducted by both women. Each seemed determine to memorize the other's facial composition, perhaps even commit it to memory. The people of the Raven shared a common belief when it came to deciphering faces. The width of one's lips, the arch of one's brow all told magnitudes of the adult and the life they had lived. Beth's lips curled up from frequent smiling and her brows lacked the arched intensity that Cara's possessed. Both had narrowing, pointed chins that commanded attention and respect. Their noses wore opposite shapes. Cara's was round and small, a button nose while Beth's was narrow and sharp like an eagle's beak. Often times it is said that such snouts on a human represent intelligence, and a great knowledge.

Cara's untamed brown hair, Beth's cropped blond mane. Cara's skin was tanned; Beth's was flushed and pink in the face, the rest a tawny white. Wolfy gold eyes, a solely human shade of ghostly blue. On one side of the tent was a women with a round face, across from her a sharp face. Each found the other equally fascinating. After mutual admiration and astonishment, it was Cara who spoke.

"Who are you people? Where-" Cara gulped for breath as a

twinge of pain struck her ribs. She inhaled to continue but stopped as she felt a painful sensation in her lungs. It was as if there was an icy fire burning inside her rib cage. She had pushed herself too hard. If she took on the shape of a wolf again, perhaps she could heal better. Simply curl up in a ball and sleep the pain and the time away. The time would heal her wounds. But she couldn't do that. She was badly wounded in a human camp. The faces were unfamiliar and she had forgotten the activity that buzzed when a group of people gathered. As a wolf, she would hardly be able to sleep. She had not been around this many people sense she left the village. But she liked it. And she was here now, attempting conversation with a woman. *Her* woman, the new character in her life.

"Where did you come from?" Cara was able to speak her words with more poise than she had expected. Still, she had struggled to shape the words coming out of her mouth. She must have sounded retarded. Regardless, Cara followed up her question with a hacking cough that brought up blood and made both women wince.

"What have you done to yourself? Sshh...Don't talk for now. Just listen. I'll explain where you are and who we are. But don't worry; no harm will come to you from us." Beth eased Cara back down and threw an additional blanket on her. This one was hand nit and seemed as soft as it was sturdy.

"Here. Drink this." Beth handed Cara a canteen filled with a pungent smelling drink inside. She drank the beverage and felt the same burning sensation down her throat as she did in her lungs. Within moments though, her pain was gone. The alcohol had done its trick. Drinking more than needed, Cara gulped down the liquor that had brought back memories of her and Bill. Often they drank strong drinks that burned the belly on cold nights. The inner warmth made them smile, and brought them closer together. In her vulnerable state, she missed him inalienably. She needed to feel his massive strength around her, protecting her, to make her whole once again. For the first time Cara felt alone. She knew she would be strong again if only she could curl up into his arms and rest again.

After watching her patient drain the liquor from the canteen, Beth took a swing from a jar she had brought up for herself. Then, she smiled and went on to speak.

"My name is Beth. I don't know where I'm from anymore. None of us at this camp remember. All that we think matters is where we are, and who we are looking for. We are a group of people from many different parts of the Nation of the Raven, we all share one thing. The dream, and the vision, given to us by a great White Tiger. We-" Beth stopped to take another drink. The alcohol had a strong taste that bit Beth's tongue and made her squeeze her eyes tight and shake her head as she swallowed it down. Across from her Cara was sitting up and laughing, even though it pained her. Ignoring Cara's reactions, Beth continued.

"We are looking for the Harvest valley and in it, the woman who lives there. Can you even understand me?" Beth realized then that perhaps her patient spoke a different tongue. She had struggled to speak when she asked Beth a question and back on the mountain she spoke in unshaped growls and howls. Though she had once told her to hush, now Beth longed to hear the woman speak. Beth stared at the mangled patient, waiting for her to reply.

"What's the woman's name?" Cara asked with a sly grin. Even in times of pain, she managed to retain her sense of humor in full. Like the wolf's brother coyote, Cara often played the trickster.

"Her name is Cara Sedalia." Beth let out a sigh of relief, the woman understood her completely.

"Do you know what, Beth?" Cara felt her heart beat increase as she anticipated the shock her answer would give Beth. She just looked at Cara, with a questioning look on her face. Beth was wise like the deer within and held the silence in wait. She was not the type to pounce for information, the doe was far to docile, and a prey animal, not a hunter for response

"My name is Cara Sedalia, though I haven't heard it spoken in full for quite some time." Beth's mouth gaped open and Cara laughed and coughed in amusement. It was a shock to her too, for these were indeed *her* people. The missionaries from her dreams. The time of discovery had arrived. It was just not expected that she would find them like this.

Sitting opposite of her, Beth sat as if she were stunned. Her eyes had grown wide and a shiver raced through her body, from fingers to toes. Beth could not believe it. No wonder she had felt so drawn to this strange woman! This person in front of her, this creature, sitting naked, battered and bruised was to become the leader of her and her group.

It had never been more needed, for the camp had been struggling to maintain its structure and balance. Fights had been occurring more often and the darker traits of humanity had put most members in ill graces with another. Betrayal, lies and greed. Now they had no leader or guide. The camp was still set up nightly though the attending members varied from night to night. Was she really to believe that Cara could change all this? Self doubt was one of the darkest traits a human can poses and luckily, Cara possessed none. It was obvious. Beth believed in her. If she could challenge death and win, she could certainly reel in the mistreated members of her tribe.

"The Harvest valley is not far off, Beth. Let me rest for another day and then I will take you and my people back to my home. I am so happy, and I want to meet them all but I would like to recover a bit first." With that Cara crawled under the blankets and peered out at Beth. There was so much more Beth wanted to know, she was fascinated and it took her breath away. Although looking at Cara, she was clearly in need of rest. Cara had found them at last; she was their prophecy, their savior.

"Thank you, Cara. I will go tell everyone in the camp of you. They will all be so excited; we have been traveling to find you for many seasons. And the White Tiger, he has shared with us visions of the life that awaits us. What are the labs like?"

"Labs?" Cara opened her eyes in alarm. What was Beth talking about?

"Oh never mind. I'm sorry Sedalia. I will be up to check on you in the morning. We can talk then, if you feel up to it anyway. Until then, sleep well. We have dogs with us that will protect you fro the wolves and bears. We are all as safe as can be. Oh and there is a dagger by your feet. Just in case."

"The animals of the forest are nothing to fear here, Beth. That is the first thing your people need to know. They are all my friends, so please be sure not to harm any of them. Understood?" Cara hadn't meant to sound so harsh. She hadn't been around humans in so long that she forgot how fragile they could be. Luckily, Beth had a beast inside who was specifically submissive to Cara's wolf. Beth would understand that pain and exhaustion had altered her tone, only to signify the importance of her words.

"I understand Cara, we do not believe in harming our brothers and sisters of the wilds. I was just trying to comfort you, but should have chosen my words better. Oh, and the dagger is in case of trouble with the humans, lately they have not been listening to their inner creatures. They are not like you and I..." With that, Beth stood up and exited the tent. For a moment her profile was outlined by the contrasting shades of darkness inside and the glow of fire outside. She was very slim and pointy, but from the glow of her face she was well fed. Or perhaps she was just drunk. either way, she had seen Cara's wolf, and the mentioning of more shifters exciting Cara like a child waiting a summer play day. She hadn't felt this way in quite some time, everything was falling into place. Everything except Beth's comment about a lab. *Oh well, I will find out in the morning.* Was Cara's final conscious thought as sleep wrapped around her like the arms of her lover, warming and cradling her into a calm state of rest.

****

Riding with Agility always brought Whispering Bill a feeling of wholeness. Always except for now. As he rode through the forest he kept an eye out for any sign of Cara. He missed her tonight, and felt as if something must be wrong. Perhaps nothing was wrong but at the very least, he knew he did not like it. The wind blew differently, the woods were loud with creatures stirring in the bliss of spring, and then there were the trees. The trees mocked his imagination by making shapes of both wolf and woman. It was driving him mad.

Agility sensed his anxiety and broke from her gallop into a run; she was taking a trail made by the wolves. She had never followed the trail to it's end so as their destination remained unknown. Alas, with her new speed the trees quit their game with Agility's mount and piece of mind made its way back to Bill.

After a few moments of riding, without warning, Bill forced her into a halt. He saw something, and it scared him. It was in front of them, in midst of the aged pines. Agility let out a snort of hot breath that made a puff in the air. Bill did not speak. What he saw was a giant building unlike any he or his people had ever made. It was unlike anything he had ever seen before and it smelled like cold, clean stone. Nothing like the cedar-scented dwellings he was accustomed to.

Fifteen
~~~~~~~~~~~~~~~~~~~~~~~~~~~~~~~~~~

Fear and confusion struck Bill like an anvil, pulling him to the ground where he began to shift. Looking at the establishment through the eyes of a bear was no help, except for now he felt stronger and secure. Agility swished her tail, remaining alert and waiting for some kind of que from the grizzly. As Bill reared onto his hind legs and lifted his nose to the air, Agility flared her nostrils, attempting to take in the scent. The bear's nose wiggled but found no new purchase of scent in the air. He lowered his paws to the ground with a thump. He looked back at the white mare and watched for her to give chase. When she did not, Bill turned his hunting eyes away from her, she was not prey. When power pulsed through him it had a way of controlling his psyche and allowing the predator to take over. The great brown bear lumbered towards the structure, each limb as thick and heavy as a tree trunk. In the background, Agility just stood and watched.

The bear found nothing that marked the tall stone walls, no scent, no claw marks claiming the building. After circling the structure he arrived at the doors, though he found nothing again. Not even the smells of nature had seeped into the walls. It was completely neutral and thus, very confusing. Laying flat on the forest floor, Bill rubbed his muzzle in the dirt, flopping his head from side to side like a carp fish. In the middle of his display, his round ears pricked. Bouncing to his hind legs, muzzle still dark with earth, he swung his head in all directions until he targeted the noise. It was directly behind him, and it sounded again. Beautiful female laughter. Bill dropped down and swiveled to face his audience.

"Had enough, Whispering Bill Harrington?" and as the women spoke Bill's name, his body responded in such a way that caused his body to change and put his spirit back into a human shell.

The woman who had spoken was leaning against a skinny evergreen with her arms folded and a wide smile on her face. Her skin was olive, her eyes were as dark as her hair, and it fell wildly on her shoulders as a mix of kinks and braids and curls. She was neither old or young but her body sparkled like the night sky that shone above them. She was cleverly clad in a gown of knit and bird feathers. It looked so colorful and fit her snugly, yet she seemed perfectly comfortable.

It was then that Bill became aware of his own attire, rather, his lack of attire. He had on nothing. It was then that made him grateful for the patches of hair that grew on his human body. They at least helped to disguise his more vulnerable parts and, they tried to keep him warm against the cool night winds.

"My dearest son, where is your mate? Is she not with you on your adventure tonight?" It all made sense, her identity rushing to him with undeniable force. This woman was his mother, the gypsy that held Jack's heart. Only a spirit could sparkle and charm a grizzly into human shape with such grace. And now she asked about Cara. Did she not know where she was either? What did he dare say? With his response, he could only hope his mother would approve.

"I am alone tonight mother. My mistress, my lady, my wolf is as wild as the wind. She goes where she pleases, but always comes back to me." Bill wanted ask more from his mother. Where was his father? Why was she here? And what was this place he and his mare had stumbled upon?

"Cara has a spirit envied even by me. But she will come back to you, my flesh." Bill eased a bit, hearing that his mate would be returning sounded good. Even though the details of her whereabouts were not spoken of, it still felt good.

"I can't help but smile as I look at you, my son. You have grown into quite the man and, quite the beast. Even the great Tiger would take notice your presence. I am so proud." She began to walk towards Bill, each step chiming from the bells strung around her ankles. She stopped a foot away from him, and he could smell her rich fragrance. It was like sweet incense and sage, as he realized her had smelled her presence in the past. With her this close, he felt his answers even closer. Thus, he had to ask,

"What is this place, mother?" The gypsy took in a deep breath and smiled, flashing a gold canine tooth.

"This is the building for Cara and her people. It is not finished, but it will be by the time *she* discovers it. Oh and don't worry tonight, she is on her way. She is injured, but she has found her people and will be bringing them with her. It won't be tonight, but they will return soon. This is where they will conduct research and gain knowledge to protect our earth. They will give the world outside of NOTR the gift of their compassion and knowledge. Tell this to Cara when you see her again. She will already know but will be comforted to hear my words from your mouth. I find it difficult to talk to her, her spirit is stronger than mine and only the tiger can seem to get the message across to her. If it were not for him, she would just do what she feels. She would have never endured the struggles to get to you.

She did not know what true love was until she met you."

"Neither would I, mother. She is the sweetest form of bliss I have ever felt. But, you made her fall in love with me?

"No my son, not even the Tiger can make one fall in love. She loved you the moment she saw you but with our world so new to her at the time, I was unsure if she would follow her heart or her mind. She is my gift to you. I wanted your love to strengthen her in this valley, and aid her in the trials that await her. So perhaps it is not so much that I brought her to you, as I brought *you* to *her*." Bill was speechless. What could one say to all that?

"Go back home my son. Visit with the wolves, wait for your darling. Oh and one more thing-" She stepped foreword and placed a braceleted hand on Bill's broad muscle-ripped shoulder. He felt like there were birds wildly flapping and flying inside of him. The warmth from her closeness prickled on his skin, as if he was thawing out from some fierce cold. He allowed his eyes to drift down and meet hers; waiting for the last thing his mother had to say.

The gypsy let strong words out of her delicate mouth as she said,

"Our horses look good." and then with a blink, she was gone.

****
*

With Beth tending to her every need, Cara made a timely recovery. She also learned much about the people she was brought to. She was to be their guide, leader, chief and alpha. From the two nights she had spent sitting aside the fire, she had heard many different tales of just what it was that awaited them upon their arrival to the valley. A place for knowledge to grow, from there it must be spread and shared. That was a popular verse members of camp told her. Some even chanted it during an evening camp-side music session.

Of the tribe, all the men and women were exceedingly kind and intelligent creatures. In each human Cara saw the face of a beast behind their eyes. Each night the camp was wild and busy with activity. Creatures loped and bounded through the brush, owls and night hawks traced figures in the night sky. It seemed that these people were not as different from her as she had once thought.

There were dogs that guarded the camp, just as Beth had said.

They pulled sleds and patrolled the camp for sign of intruders or prey. Cara had come to notice however, that these dogs would not speak to her, even though some looked exceptionally wolfish. Perhaps they were being odd. Or perhaps they could not understand her. Way they worked hard and she enjoyed traveling with dogs again, the days with Jack had been hard but the adventures and the bond with the dogs had been well worth it.

It was bright one particular night as Cara sat alone in an empty creek bed. Summer was close at hand. The warm season was pulling the sun up into the sky, even when it would be at rest in other parts of the country. It hit the moon with the fullest of its radiance once it disappeared and made the moon shine. That was why, Cara explained to herself, tonight was so bright.

Cara picked up a smooth river pebble and rolled it in her palm. Doing so she also had a chance to examine her coordination. She seemed to be recovering well. Her legs had bruises; her arms bore deep cuts that were healing into thick lines of scabs and scares. The power of recovery, it was beautiful. Time and time again she cursed her poor human composition. Too fleshy, too naked. It was hard to go a day without breaking the fragile skin that covered her muscle and bones. But tonight is seemed that what breaks easily can heal as easily in return favor. That was nice.

She was sitting in the creek bed, counting her wounds when she heard the pack sing to her. Being in company with people and away from them she had forgotten the vicious mix of emotions that stirred inside of her when hearing Risk's call. It was even more intense now. He was growing up, an adult in her eyes and soon, if not already, he would be searching for a mate. From the strain in his howl, Cara sensed that she was perhaps not the only thing Risk was calling for.

The rest of the pack joined in. Granite first, shrieking Rage and at last the quivering call of Aqua. His voice still sounded young. The consequences of being an omega at an early age. Cara wanted to howl back though she held it inside of her, behind clenched teeth.

Staring at the half moon she felt the irony of seeing her reflection in the sky. She was the half moon, always fighting to maintain her balance. The light and the dark, making a perfect circle and an icon in the evening canvas. Her selfish side wanted nothing more than to rip out of her cloths and run off towards the sound of her pack. The bright side, the side that shone for others to see was her human face that held her new tribe together. She would guide them to a garden of knowledge in the Harvest valley below. *They* were her new pack.

Cara found the balance when she called back to Risk in response, but did not get up to move. She had things to do; she had people who needed her. It just so happened that she was still human enough to harbor the labor of responsibility and guilt. So for another night she stayed because she felt she belonged with them every bit as much as she did with the pack, if not more.

After three days of travel and counsel, Cara and the travelers finally approached the valley. For Cara, the return home was magnificent. It was dusk, her favorite time of day. The world around her was teetering between the farewell of the day and the dawning of the night. From the valley below, Cara heard the pack's voices rise up in greeting. It made her heart jump and her pace increase. She walked down the mountain with Beth and a few others she had grown particularly close to, at her side.

Behind them the rest of the tribe and two sled teams followed carrying tents and food and supplies. Each member of the camp wore a pack. They were a very well prepared group, Cara had to admit. Being around so many blond and brown strangers made her realize the simplicity of her travels. She had gone very far without carrying very much. Even now she wore only enough to keep her warm and decent in the company of others. If it weren't for the pack and their food, traveling strength, protection, and warmth, she would have died within weeks. Perhaps even days.

The terrain began to level itself out as the final hill descended into the grassy plains of the valley. Home. The horses were out in the pasture though the house looked quiet in all its distance. Then, all of a sudden, Cara saw something flash in the western forest. She didn't know why she passed the cabin but the wolves weren't there and she saw no sign of Bill. As they crossed the meadow, patched with dry tundra, Cara whistled for Dusty to aid her in her journey.

The magnificent golden steed came galloping towards her in dazzling glory. It was as if he had been but hoof prints near her rather than the hundreds of yards back, where he was enjoying the budding flowers hidden in the thickets. Spirit horses were gifted in such ways. After pressing his soft nose on her neck, arms, legs and revealed stomach, Dusty bowed down so that Cara could mount him with relative ease. From nuzzling her skin and listening to her heartbeat, he could tell that Cara was injured and accommodated her as best he could.

Racing ahead of the hikers, Dusty ran to where he had seen Agility and Bill disappear to last. He had watched them ride, and had yet to see Bill's return. Agility had been back, but spoke nothing of their travels. Dusty knew he should take Cara to him. For the past two days, the herd had been dining on the valley's abundance of late spring and drinking from the cool lake as usual.

As Cara curled her fingers deeper into Dusty's sun drenched mane, she found it intriguing that the direction she was headed in was towards the mysterious flash she had seen when coming down the hill. Her heart beat with vigor. The thrill of Dusty's ride, the anticipation of what awaited her in the woods, the mystery of her mate's disappearance and over all, fear pumped her blood hot inside of her.

Cara howled. The pack did not respond. She and Dusty were moving deeper and deeper into the woods. It was as dark as the seasons would permit and the people would want to set up camp soon. That she knew. Or would they help themselves to her cabin? Her question was answered by the bone-rattling, mind shaking sound of a grizzly's throaty roar. Then voices, screaming and yelling. All this was occurring a few acres of woods away. Though her legs were weak and heavy, Cara managed to kick Dusty in the side; he had stopped and was too spooked to move. But with her kick, he began to blitz in the direction of the commotion. They were on their way.

Sixteen
~~~~~~~~~~~~~~~~~~~~~~~~~~~

Listening through the pounding of hooves and her own heart, Cara heard the bear roar once more. It was like dynamite exploding. She was surprised there were not trees crashing down around the sound. In response she heard humans speaking in midst of their yells and chants. What were they saying? Cara strained her ears to find out. On any quieter night she would have been able to hear and understand but tonight, the forest was far too alive with noise. Her senses were overloaded and busy taking in the magnitudes of sights, smells and sounds. It didn't help that she was aching and exhausted either.

A flash went off and in the darkness that it left her blinded in, it took her a moment to realize that her horse had stopped and the bear was but a few feet away. He was an adult male, huge and hairy. His shaggy fur glistened in the moonlight as he snorted his fury and nosed at the loose dirt beneath him. Cara's shoulders dropped when she saw that it was Bill. His presence here brought a sense of relief. She had not recognized his growl earlier. Ears pressed flat in fear, Dusty let his young years get the best of him as he dropped his belly to the ground. Sedalia cursed, and got off the horse. She rubbed his neck, smoothing the hairs that seemed to be standing on end. Turning around she realized all the voices, all the people, had disappeared. Causing her own hairs to stand on end.

Figures flickered like flames amidst the trees. Eyes that shone bright as stars flashed in the coal dark woods and they were located all around her. Humans, owls, bears, bats, cats, deer, elk, caribou, coyotes, wolves, foxes, moose, horses, raccoons, badgers, eagles, otters, voles and hares. Creatures off all caliber surrounded Cara and Bill. Stepping closer until they touched, Cara ran her hand deep into her Kodiak's coat. This was what had him so upset, or was there something more?

Looking up at her from his round, teddy bear eyes, Bill got inside of her head. *Follow Me.* She wanted to shift; she needed to feel the healing powers of the change and to be able to communicate easier with Whispering Bill. She had missed him and loved him so, and in a time of exposure and over-stimuli such as this, she knew she needed him. But she couldn't release, she couldn't change. It was as if her body had forgotten how. Focusing her mind frame, she blocked out her fear and pain. That was all she could do. Leaving the golden colt alone, side by side the woman and the grizzly trudged through the wilderness in quest of the unknown.

They plowed through the flame-dancing shadow figures in the woods. Each watched them preceded, but made no faces of threat or attack. Within a short acre, the bear brought Cara to the massive building he had previously discovered. It was snuggled away in the forest so well that Cara could not even see it from the top of the cliff. And it was from there, after all, that she thought she could see everything. Touching Bill on the soft of his snout, Cara walked away from him and towards the doors of the massive establishment. Fear was too inconsequential to hold her back. Pulling with minimal effort on the doors, Cara found that they opened easily. Her eyes rolled back in her head. This was becoming too familiar. Black out.

****

Cara came into consciousnesses with her feet hitting the ground. Literally. One-two-three-four-one-two-three-four. That was the rhythm she carried. This beat was not the familiar two-step walking pace she often carried. Looking down, watching the moving earth beneath her, ocular senses discovered her vessels of transportation were not the human feet she had been born with and come to accept. Beneath her ran silver furred wolf legs, ending in wide spread paws. Slowing her pace to further study herself, she overcame her shock and surprise and realized these were indeed her own paws. Four toes and a dew claw stretched and wiggled at her command. Unaware and unconcerned with how she came to be this way, she stretched out the tendons in her thighs as she prepared for a lengthy uphill trot. Where she was, she could not tell. Though as she proceeded up the slope she came to understand that the wolf had taken over. She did not care, she let it.

Coming into her wolf body had never been hard, never a struggle, never anything other than amazing. The feeling was that of ecstasy and relief, like a burden had been lifted from her. Like an itching had been soothed. In the most vulgar of her own terms, running as a wolf was like finally finding a place to pee after holding it for far too long. It was relief that took away stresses from her mind and body. The change was also something she had longed for from the earliest stages of existence. Growing up she often spoke to her parents about her fantastic ideas to live as anything other than human. Shifting to her wolf body was like justice finally served. Her first life struggles finally rewarded. Shifting into a wolf, Cara finally felt that she was one of her own kind.

Five suns and four moons had past by when Cara, still in her wolf body, had a moment of conscious where upon she pondered her current state and surroundings. She had blacked out, injured, as a human. That was the last she could recall even as she pressed her brain for further details. The faces, the images, from the adventures with Beth, the canyon, the pack, and returning to find Bill as a bear rolled through her head like the movies Cara had once seen in the villages with Ol' Jack.

  Was all that really real? Was she really there? Was that really her? What happened? Why wasn't she home and where was she? A crisp breeze tickled the family of aspen trees the wolf was resting under. They rattled like an infant's toy and made her loose her train of thought.

  As it were, a shape shifter is a being that can shift their mental or physical state of existence into another form. Altering consciousness, trancing out, mantras, it all can open up a wide selection of opportunities. It is said however, by the wisest elders of the oldest tribes across the nations, that if a shifter lingers in one form for too long, they will loose the ability to shift back. With that in mind, Cara had "gone wolf" for over two weeks. Thoughts of Bill, the camp, her home, even her pack had faded away to become no more than a hazy recollection until now.

  Precise geographical location still remained a mystery to her as well. There were aspens, pines, spruces and elms. Scattered throughout them was the majestic blue spruce, native to and most commonly seen in the mountains of Colorado. The air was too dry and thin to be that of her previous existence in NOTR. In addition, the sun was too hot and the game was too scarce to be anywhere ear the Harvest Valley. Rabbits and marmots had become her main prey while the occasional fallen mule deer was a splendid addition to her diet. Day and night she traveled. Cara rarely slept, pushing herself so hard that her tongue would flicker with the speed of a hummingbird's unstoppable wings. The silver wolf was always searching. Looking, exploring and traveling unknown trails to find something she could not fathom. She had been human too long and ignored her body's urge to shift, forcing it to take over. Now the majority of her mind had been wolf for far too long and her brain didn't dare to comprehend more than survival techniques and skills. She could not seem to handle anymore, though in the back of her mind the thoughts still lingered there. Somethings one cannot ignore.

  It was the rising of her second full moon in this strange land. A sad sound of desperation hinted in her echoing howls that night. Never was there a response other than silence. Nothing from a coyote, rarely from an owl and once from a cougar many days ago. She was definitely no longer in the arctic. She was in cat country and tonight, they were all out.

  Lynx, cougars and bob cats left their mark throughout the many miles the she-wolf had traveled. The scent of their urine and musk curled Cara's lips up and force her to bite her tongue between her teeth. It had rained during the day of the second full moon. Past-due moisture brought life to the plants, and life to the creatures that ate them. With all the deer and elk out and active, it pulled all the feline predators from their trees and dens to the meadows and hills to hunt. Cara was no where near a river and instead of hunting the newly migrated deer, the she-wolf hunted for water.

The search was an all-night affair and not so much as a pool of collected rain water revealed itself. It was a desperate time and forced Cara to lick the morning dew from fallen yellow leaves. It would be considerable to presume that what occurred in her mind was due to her current state of famine. Either way, the new day brought remembrance and new meaning to the she-wolf's life. Lying down allowing thought to concur her, Cara felt the deep throbbing of loneliness inside of her. She licked her silky grey fur with a long, pink tongue to reassure herself of no physical injury. There was none. Only the emotional ache of loneliness. Cara was tired of being alone. She missed Bill, missed the humans, even missed *being* human. The past few nights and days reminded her that nature could still be cruel.

What she wanted now, she wanted more than water. She wanted to talk, to hear someone's voice, speaking to her. She wanted to be touched and held. She wanted to feel to softness of a knit blanket, wrapped around her as she slept. And her pack. What any wolf, or what any human for that matter, really need was their own pack. It made no difference where one "lived". One could never truly be able to "live" without someone to share life with. For even all that she had accomplished out here as a wolf, really, it meant nothing. She would have much to tell and boast about, for she was growing into her skills as a wolf. However, if she were never human again, no one would ever know.

It was with that thought that the silver wolf stood up and took a ragged breath. Looking up into the towering heights of evergreens, Cara opened her jowls for a final howl in this shape.

"Aooooooooooo!" There was regained strength and a sound of confidence in her call. It was today that Cara fully understood the balance between wolf and woman.

Turning wolf had always been the easiest part of shifting for Cara. It was shifting back that occasionally presented a problem, like her body resisted. Normally she would step into one body then out into another but, today, she felt stuck. It took an understandable amount of physical and mental effort to will herself into another change. Cara's body was resisting the return to a bi-ped state, it had been to long. Her brain however, was swelling with the flooding of thoughts and emotions that were simply incompatible with a wolf's intelligence. Basic principals of emotion were easy. It was things like background stories and elaborates details that didn't make it in. Though the pressure in her mind helped. Before shifting back was almost unfathomable but today it was not only possible, it was the answer.

After feeling sensations like that of legs being shredded by dull, thorny branches repeatedly, the change was complete. Naked and exhausted, Cara felt her ears pop as a final adjustment to her beautiful, naked form. She was still very thirsty but sleep called her and claimed her first. The warm daylight sun filtered in through the pines. It never hit her eyes and so she curled up in a fetal shape, sleeping 24 hours away. The night came and went and it was the morning chatter of birds that woke her the next day.

Stretching in her new, though familiar, skin, bones popped and clicked as if talking back from their own lengthy time of unused existence. Standing, Cara scratched the light fuzz on her stomach. From where she was standing she could see two paths. Around yet another hill, into thick brush and woods or, up a different hill littered with budding thorny bushes. Listening, she could hear crows calling together a congregation. The had found something. food or water didn't matter. They were over the hill and that was where Cara was going.

Instincts were rewarded as she downed the steep hill covered in pines, boulders and brush. To keep from loosing her footing, Cara made her way down the hill holding on to a tree at a time. Twice though the damp earth, still covered in shadows, slid from beneath her and each time she slid ungracefully until she lost her momentum and fell with a thud onto her butt. Switching reflexes had left her a bit clumsy still. It added to her frantic pace that coming down the hill, she could hear rushing water not too far way. Once the slope finally died down into flat land, Cara raved through the forest kicking up stones and twigs and she fled.

The forest opened up gradually, as it so often does, no matter where you go. The endless sea of trees died down to clumps, with those dwindling down to a sparse few staggering timbers. The blue spruce trees seemed to enjoy lingering by such a large body of water for as Cara approached, she not only saw the massive, gushing river, but she saw lines of blue spruces and tall grasses that had found good purchase in the soil. Smooth, round boulders reminded Cara of over sized stepping stones as she approached. Coming to the stream's edge, Cara waded in a half a foot and bent down into the pulling current to drink. The cold water tasted like gold, or if gold were to be a desirable taste. Either way, she drank until she could feel her stomach fill and then forced herself to pull back to prevent lurching up that which she had just drank.

Seventeen
~~~~~~~~~~~~~~~~~~~~~~~~~

A large rock that had gone flat on it's top made for an ideal resting spot, it seemed. It hung over the river, though off to the side where a slow-moving pool had formed. Climbing up the heated rock Cara saw that the stilling water beneath her made for a perfect dipping hole. The boulder even slanted down into the water, as if to make a slide, just for her. Her skin had been uncovered, and had collected plenty of dust, scrapes, stench and mud to pull her into the water before her nap. Easing in her toes, the water was cold and chilled her in a way that made her smile. Were she wolf, she would not feel the smoothness of the water that chilled her. Skin that was so naked, skin that was so sensitive even simple sensations gave her pleasure.

Sliding into the water she plunged herself down to find the floor of the pool. The cold made her body scream to get out and get air, but she was enjoying the smooth pebbles of the river. Touching the bottom brought her legs to a depth that brought a deeper feeling of cold. With that, she kicked frantically to reach the surface. She did not want to overestimate her body and freeze.

Hopping onto the sandbar, her skin rippled with chills. It was of little matter, she felt clean and refreshed. Kneeling down to the ground, her knees plunged into sepia-colored mud. Cara drove her hands into the mud, pulling out cold, red clay and mushing it between her fingers and throwing it like a child at play. For the first time in a month, she heard herself laugh. She was happy this day. Soon, hunger would come back and perhaps even bring on fear. For now however, joy ruled the day. After smearing the red clay on her face and body, Cara climbed back atop the flat boulder. Spread-eagle, she gazed up at the cloudless sky. The sun began to cook her hair and skin. It made her feel warm, inside and out and pushed her into another long nap.

Opening her sleepy eyes, Cara saw the clear night sky. Above her, the yellow sun had been replaced with a big, round moon gleaming back at her in all its fullness. Flipping from her back to her stomach, she slid down the boulder and onto the sandbar beneath her. Ten toes squished into the mud while her heels stayed off the ground. Still adjusting from the change, it was easiest to walk this way, and quieter as well. Hunger and curiosity drove her to explore. Following the river she walked until she came into a clearing where she saw two figures, less than fifty feet away. Farthest from her was a deer, ears fully cupped with eyes that were wide and alert. Just behind it, closest to Cara, was a massive white tiger. Crouching and ready to make a kill. The feline was huge, with stripes as thick as Cara's own knee.

Hushing her breath, Cara took two steps back, using all efforts to remain silent. She did not want to disturb this predator and have his blood lust target her instead of his current pursuit. Either way it was too late, all her efforts were wasted. The doe swung her head to sight Cara, and it took off. Readying his haunches for the leap, the tiger took one monstrous bound that easily covered twenty feet. Front legs reached out, claws extended, the tiger latched onto his prey as they both came tumbling down into the tall grass. Lying flat as a board, Cara watched and listened as the great white tiger tore open the flesh of the deer with one effortless bite. Tail whipping in the air, he began to feed. All Cara could do was watch, and wait.

After a lengthy while of appetizing gore, the great beast withdrew from the deer and licked his paws. He was done, cleaning the carcass down to the bone. Cara's fingers dug into the dirt as if she still had her claws. Her eyes had been glued to the uncomprehendable magnificence of the tiger. After a session of grooming, cleaning the blood from his face and body, the tiger lifted his head and studied his surroundings. The banging beat of her heart seemed to be silenced when the tiger began to look her way. He saw her. Through teal blue eyes, his gaze was steady and unreadable. The cat's ears did not shift, his tail did not move. What would happen next could be anything from death to injury to an uninterested look and a harmless departure.

The moon was brighter than a spotlight. It cast it's silver glow on every piece of grass in the sea between them. A cool breeze drifted

over Cara and made the grass ripple in waves. As good as the cool
night air felt, it managed to steal her breath as it carried her scent
directly into the nostrils of the tiger. Even without her pack, Cara was
not the type to cower. She had seen this tiger before, but it was the
great power that he possessed that made her leery. Pushing up with
her arms, Cara lifted herself slowly so as not to startle the beast.
When she stood tall with every inch of her 5'9 height, the tiger rose
from his place of sitting and began to stride her way.

    He came to her with the gentleness of a lamb. With thick
shoulders that met level with her breasts, he circled her and brushed
up against her like a kitten. Cara smiled, both to show her teeth and
from astounded pleasure from the kindness of a killer. He spoke to
her in the way that most animals did, not in verbs and adjectives, not
with vocal speech, but a transfer of messages into her mind. The very
words that came to her, made her tremble with their awesome power
and infliction. The great white tiger, one of the strongest spirit guides
in all of the known worlds and realms, had come to her multiple
times. But never like this, never revealed in tangible physical form. It
was then that, through pride an honor, she unearthed another myth
she had held about herself. She *was* different. She was *truly* powerful
and possessed wisdom that she had never truly embraced, despite her
life long compliments and admiration.

    Warm sandpaper rolled over her left wrist, and stroked each
one of her delicate fingers. Pushing her arm up, he dove into her eyes
with a dazzling intensity that few beasts of men could ever dare to
match. Teal eyes asked, with no controlling force, for her to climb
atop his back. He wished to travel, and take *her* with *him*. She
couldn't believe it. After the weeks in primal solitude, to come back to
human life, and be greeted and possessed by a ruler of the Spirit
lands. Even as a wolf she would not refuse. Questions still lingered
about where she was and how she came to be in this warp of time and
place. Climbing on his back, it didn't seem to matter. Wherever she
was, wherever she had been, was of little importance. It had died into
the past and she was not dead. What mattered was what was alive,
she was alive, and riding off into the future was birth to a new
adventure, the purest example of living.

    Cara's fingers were clinched into the thick, bristly fur of the
tiger. His feet hit the ground with almost an inaudible padding as he
increased his trot into a gallop. Soon his gallop turned into a run, his
run bursting into a full out sprint. The speed the animal reached was

practically dizzying, until it became mind numbing. All she could comprehend were the colors blazing by them, and the thrash of wind as they tore through the air and further into the balmy night.

Pulling her head into the shallow dome between the tiger's shoulders, she squeezed him tight and laid her head to one side for further aerodynamics. The dark blues and grays of the shadowy plains swirled together until it seemed they were no longer existent. There was color no longer. Instead it ass faded into a creamy, glittering white. She had never seen any vision like it, not even when smoking the pipe with Whispering Bill. Her attention came to her hands, sweaty with adrenaline and nerves, they were slipping. Cara dug into his fur further, curling into skin. Wincing, afraid she caused the tiger pain, she shut her eyes and tightened her legs around the cat.

Eighteen
~~~~~~~~~~~~~~~~~~~~~~~~~~~~~

When she dared to reopen her eyes, she was back at home, in front of the same structure she had passed out in front of. The beast had stopped and she could feel the steady rise and fall of his ribcage, obviously catching his breath. Cara was stunned. She lay there, pressed against the giant tiger in shock. She now felt the considerable change in temperature, and the cold made her flesh ripple and rise in tiny bumps. The great cat turned his heavy-weight head back towards her. He intended for her to get off of him. She responded quickly, though reluctant to feel the chill of the ground on her bare feet. She had adjusted to the mild temperatures of wherever it was she had been for so long. Stepping of, she began to feel her body shake, and not from the cold. Her arms and legs seemed to rattle from the momentum of their returning ride.

"Go inside Cara. This place is yours. It is a laboratory, a home for your people, and a sanctuary for both you and your people. Someday it will even serve as sanctuary to a wild creature."

Cara was too awed to respond, she could hardly even mover her head to look around. It would have done her no good, for there was no one else there. Just her, a long haired woman, lost in time, scarred from living and wide eyed at the potential of this new gift. Reaching out her hand, she clasped the cool handle of the left main door. There were two, side by side. Made from wood and rock and glass. There was some other material; she was slightly unfamiliar with it until the word for it came. Metal.

Cara stepped into a wide hallway, a lobby, with multiple doors on both sides and light shining from the end. It was a rustic version of what she, as a child, had been told heaven would be like. The thought of that forced image from her distant past brought a smile to her face. Behind her, the white tiger padded into the walkway, stopping beside her. He tilted his view to capture her once again. Eyes the color of a spring beneath a glacier motioned for her to explore. As she did, her promised began to explain.

Treading lightly, as if her footsteps would destroy the impeccable look of cleanliness from the polished stone beneath her, she began to walk to hallway. She stopped at her first door on her left. This door was simple in design, a push door made of wood. The open door revealed a large oblong-shaped common room. About half the size of the home she shared with Bill. It was furnished with tables, two kitchens and other indoor luxuries. In the center was a fire pit, as was custom in the resides from civilians of the Nation of the Raven. The ceiling was low, no more than ten feet from the ground and a slideable slat of metal created an escape for the smoke of the fire. Exploring the interior of the room, Cara came across two sets of double doors. One set led out into the woods. The next, she pushed through to conquer that witch way behind them.

Another hallway, though far more narrow than the main lobby. To the right were concealed wash basins and bathrooms and mirrors to as well. The seemed to be hidden from the hallway as well as hidden from bordering units. Such architectural design was brilliant, and clearly inhuman. Passing through the hygiene area, the narrow hallway emptied out back into the main lobby. Skylights let the moonlight pour in and seemed to put a glow throughout the entire house, or whatever it was.

At this point, she was not yet halfway through the lobby but the doors on the left were no more than seven feet apart. Each door, opening into a well furnished doom, suitable for two to four people. Cara sped past them, there seemed to be around twenty of them, ten on each side. It appeared that the building was symmetrical, a duplicate center room and bathroom lobby was on the left side of the building as well. The doors to the dorm stopped and were replaced with wider, thick doors, much further apart.

On one side, was the lab the cat had mentioned. It was packed with what appeared to be all types of scientific goodies. Much of what she saw was new to her, but the tiger assured her of their use to her people. Some were biologists, scientist, mathematicians, chemists and doctors. All hailing from somewhere, or sometime in the Nation of the Raven. The lab branched off into what was surely meant to be a hospital. A place to care for people and for wounded or billed animals. Exiting that chamber, Cara was prepared to cross the hall and reveal whatever it was that came next.

Striding past her, the cat preceded her entrance, preparing to explain the unfamiliar contents inside. This sect was a filming room, an editing booth, an outlet to the rest of the world and nations. It would be under strict circumstances that communication was to be made outside of NOTR. Computers, internet, foreign words and terms to Cara existed here. This was where research and knowledge would be harvested and released. It was with this that the Tiger turned to Cara and spoke.

"I have one last thing to show you. Then I need to speak to you further. Come."

He took her to the end of the hallway witch opened out into the woods once more. A hundred feet from the exit were, what the tiger called, SATECTs. SATEC stood for: Study and Testing Environmental Closed Spaces. Size varied with each enclosed space, in total there seemed to be about thirty of them. Some, she was told, were big enough to even house a wolf pack comfortably. It was here that animals would be studied, healed or taken care of until they could be haled back into the wilderness, with a better chance at survival. So this was it. Except. of course, the enclosure for the sled dogs that she had passed at the entrance to the place. Cara wrapped her arms around herself and yawned in the death of the night. With that, the beast began his speech to her.

In briefing, he told Cara that he had chosen her, all those years ago, to be the one to lead in battle against ignorance for the planet, and domestication of the soul. This place, these people, her experiences were the provided tools to be used. In the time that she was away, which turned out to be a test of self discovery, each member of the camp had been briefed of what to expect, and what to accomplish.

The goal was nothing like world piece, or higher standards for humanity. Just to replace the balance of the sites and the cities. To welcome back the wild. In short, to ignite the fire of passion that every animal had inside of them, that burned to live free, and reunite with the great earth mother as one. The task, to anyone else, would be overwhelming. But Cara had faith, wisdom, instinct, enlightenment, courage...there was no fitting word for it. Whatever it was she had *something* that set her apart and readied her for this.

With the rising of the sun, the tiger bid her farewell and good luck. With a swish of his tail, he vanished before her eyes. She stood alone, watching the yellow ball of light shift into its daylight position. Bill and the tribe would be waiting at home, this she knew. She would prepare them for the battle of peace. The challenge had begun. Smiling and laughing, Cara Sedalia turned and made her way home. She had much to do.

www.ingramcontent.com/pod-product-compliance
Lightning Source LLC
Chambersburg PA
CBHW031313280626
47169CB00018B/1259